MAKE IT UP TO ME

A PSYCHOLOGICAL THRILLER

MARK GILLESPIE

This is a work of fiction. All of the events and dialogue depicted within are a product of the author's overactive imagination. None of this stuff happened. Except maybe in a parallel universe.

www.markgillespieauthor.com

First Printing: March 2022

Cover designed by MiblArt

For Billie...X

PART 1 - LISA

1

The cigarette fell from Lisa Granger's lips as she watched the car plummet into the river.

Still a little bit drunk from the night before, Lisa was standing on the footpath situated adjacent to the river. As she watched the car go over the edge, she wasn't quite sure if she was awake or still in bed caught in the grip of an alcohol-fuelled nightmare. If so, the crash was a symbol of something else. Most likely, it was a symbol of Lisa's marriage.

She was in Clydebank, a town located on the north bank of the River Clyde in Glasgow. Lisa had no business being there at the crack of dawn. She didn't live there, didn't live anywhere near it as a matter of fact. She'd crashed at Deb Munro's place last night, a two-bedroom flat in nearby Knightswood. The two women had sat up all night with two bottles of Pinot Gris (at least) and a living room floor covered with enough sugary, processed snacks to shame a children's birthday party. They'd talked about the sinking ship (or crashing car) that was Lisa and Tommy's marriage. About the latest fight, all the previous fights and the fights to come. And no matter which way they'd approached the topic, sober or drunk, optimistic or pessimistic, the conclusion was always the same.

The marriage was over.

Lisa had gotten blissfully drunk on the neverending flow of white wine. She didn't care about tomorrow or the inevitable hangover that would see her swear off alcohol for the rest of her life. Screw it. Life owed her at least one decent high. She badgered Deb all night, asking her old friend if she still smoked weed and if so, did she have any lying around the flat to take their private party to the next level? Lisa hadn't smoked weed since she was seventeen and now as a thirty-eight-year-old woman undergoing a full-blown marital crisis, this seemed like a good time to go back and reacquaint herself with Mary Joanna. No such luck. Deb, who was into all kinds of herbal woo-woo and crystals and bizarre hippy shit, explained to Lisa that she hadn't smoked weed since her late twenties.

Damn it, Lisa thought. Still, she was going to smoke something.

She'd staggered out of the flat and walked to the corner shop at the end of Deb's street, picking up two packs of cigarettes in brandless packaging. Tommy hated it whenever she smoked at parties. *Well, screw you Tommy*. The rest of the night, Lisa and Deb smoked like they were in a laboratory taking part in a scientific experiment. They talked, devoured the Gris, ate crisps and chocolate and ordered pizza. All the while, the stereo played a best of the nineties collection, including music from Oasis, The Spice Girls, and David Gray. It was the perfect soundtrack to mourn their lost youth.

The conversation never strayed far from Tommy. Tommy the prick. Tommy the dickhead. Tommy the fucking arsehole. Lisa did most of the talking while Deb listened and sympathised with the patience of an inebriated saint.

It was around one-thirty or two o'clock when the drinking session fizzled out. The women said their good-nights and an exhausted Lisa wandered into the tiny spare room, falling face first onto a rock-hard bed. She lay there, head sinking deep into the pillow. There it was, she thought. The beginnings of a headache whispering from afar, letting her know that she was going to regret everything in the morning.

It was a rough night. Lisa slept a few hours at most, tossing and turning. Unable to switch off. At first light, she got up and crept out of Deb's flat on her tiptoes. She wasn't in the mood for any of Deb's questions about what she was going to do next about the Tommy thing. Truthfully, Lisa had no idea what she was going to do. All she wanted right now was to get a little fresh air circulating around her lungs to help combat the headache, which had turned out worse than she'd feared. All that junk food lay heavy in her stomach. How long before she was kneeling in front of the toilet to bring all that back up?

Lisa caught sight of her reflection in the hall mirror as she unlocked the front door of the flat. Her caramel brown hair was a crumpled bird's nest. After the fight with Tommy, she'd stormed out of the house wearing only a simple t-shirt and jeans combo. The garments were heavily wrinkled after she'd spent the night tossing and turning in them. Yesterday's makeup was sliding off her face.

Just walk, she thought. Something will come to you.

She set out on foot, travelling west along Dumbarton Road. As she walked, Lisa relived every beat of yesterday's fight with her shit of a husband. It was a simple back and forth for the most part. She'd accused and Tommy had denied. Voices had been raised, nothing unusual these days in the Granger household. Neither one of them had yielded until Lisa's eventual walkout.

"Bastard," she said in a croaky voice.

Even the hangover was his fault.

Lisa's head was spinning. She was in the precarious zone, dangling in between last night's session and the full-blown hangover to come. All she wanted right now was a cold pint of water with lots of ice in it. Somewhere dark to lie down.

She kept walking, trying to leave the headache in the dust. No matter how fast she walked, the headache was faster.

Lisa didn't even know what time it was. She knew it was early. *Really* early. The sun was still clawing its way towards a horizon smothered in dark clouds that drifted slowly overhead. The Glaswegian air was unusually muggy. Most likely, rain was coming.

Lisa liked the feeling of being the only person in the world. She rummaged around in her pocket, pulling out that last crumpled pack of cigarettes. Smoking with a hangover? Why not? Lisa had been a smoker in her early twenties and had loved every minute of it. Smoking helped her to concentrate. It relaxed her. It was other people's constant nagging about cancer and strokes and passive smoking that had finally persuaded her to quit.

She lit up and inhaled, reliving the all-night chatter with Deb. They'd talked for hours about Lisa's suspicions regarding Tommy's infidelity. No doubt Lisa had bored the pants off Deb, God bless her for letting a drunken pal blether on about her problems till daft o'clock at night. Deb kept reminding Lisa that she didn't know for sure that Tommy was up to no good with other women. That was true. Despite all the accusations, Lisa was no further forward than she'd been yesterday after slamming the front door and walking out.

Once a cheater, always a cheater.

But did she really believe that? It wasn't true for everyone. Some people did change, but could Tommy?

Lisa could feel it in her bones. He'd done it two years ago and confessed after several days of pressure, kind of like the pressure she was putting on now. No, the old saying was good. Once a cheater, right? Sooner or later, Lisa would get to the truth about what was going on.

She walked a little faster. Beside her, the river reeked of rotting moss. There were other putrid smells of the city jamming their way up her nostrils. Stale vomit. Piss. Exhaust fumes.

Lisa followed the narrow footpath, chain-smoking like it was an Olympic sport and she was the greatest of all time. She still didn't want to go home. To hell with that. All she wanted to do was walk and keep walking, waiting for that big something to happen that would knock things into perspective once and for all. The light would come on and reveal what was supposed to happen next.

Because right now, Lisa didn't have a clue.

She could see Tommy's face. The way his lip quivered, the way he avoided eye contact when she'd accused him outright of cheating on her. He was hiding something. He was hiding it, not willing to confess to a second bout of adultery because he knew it'd be over if she found out.

"Fucker," she hissed. The anger was swirling up inside her again. The hatred she felt for Tommy at that moment was so strong it felt like she was possessed by something unholy.

"Scumbag."

Lisa formulated a crude plan of action in her head. She wasn't due in work today so she'd buy more cigarettes at the first opportunity. Find somewhere quiet to sit. A park, somewhere she could hear the birds sing and cut herself off from the sound of people and cars and city noise. Sit on a bench and smoke. Paint her lungs black with tar. Sooner or later, the enquiring texts from Tommy would start coming in and she'd ignore every single one of them. Let him think she'd walked out for good.

Had she?

"You're home late every night," Lisa said, muttering under her breath as if Tommy was right there walking beside her. "Every single night." Even before she'd plucked up the courage to confront him last night, Tommy had mentioned something about leaving early in the morning for a meeting. He hadn't looked her in the eye, pretending instead that he was interested in the bland soap opera playing on TV.

A meeting?

Did he think she was born yesterday?

Lisa wiped a tear off her cheek. No, she wouldn't cry. Let *him* cry when she didn't come home that night. Let him be the one to freak out for a change and go through the emotional rollercoaster that had so often brought Lisa to her knees in exhaustion. He was the one who'd ruined everything. Let him suffer.

She put another cigarette in her mouth and lit up. As she put the lighter back in her pocket, Lisa heard the roar of a car engine. Sounded like somebody was hitting the accelerator too hard.

Boy racers? At this time of day?

Lisa looked straight ahead. The footpath came to an end about fifty yards away and from there, it merged with a smooth, unblemished stretch of road leading off to the right. The road cut through a residential street with a modern-looking block of flats and a few houses scattered here and there. Most likely, it led into the heart of Clydebank. But the loud vehicle sounded like it was on that road. Racing towards the river. The screaming of the engine was getting louder. Surely the car was going the wrong way?

"What the...?"

Lisa could see it now. A white car, looked like an Audi, accelerating past the houses and then the tower block as if it was trying to take off. In a matter of seconds, Lisa thought, the car would run out of road. What then? Was it going to try and squeeze its way onto the footpath?

"Idiots," Lisa said, assuming it was joyriding teenagers who'd been out all night. But the car wasn't doing hand-brake turns or performing any other stunts for that matter on the road. All it was doing was hurtling towards the water at a lethal speed.

Lisa's heart pounded in her chest.

She heard a muffled scream from inside the car. A woman's voice, accompanied by the sound of a man yelling. It was a chilling cacophony of terror. Lisa saw a flash of movement up front. Looked like there was some kind of struggle going on in the front seat and the car was jerking wildly from side to side. But it didn't stop. It only seemed to be going faster.

And it was heading straight for the river.

2

The car was metres away from the steel barrier at the water's edge. It *was* an Audi. White metallic exterior.

Everything happened so fast. Lisa saw a blur of chaotic movement inside the car. Flapping arms. The constant screaming and yelling didn't let up. The woman sounded like she was in terrible pain. The Audi had by now cleared the tower block and there was only the river left to come. The vehicle fishtailed wildly, closing in on the solid metal barrier, the last thing on the road and footpath preventing cyclists and cars from plunging into the water. But Lisa had already noticed a chink in the barrier's sturdy armour. At the end of the footpath, where it merged with the road, a strip of flimsy wire fencing had been erected. It looked like a temporary barrier, about four metres in width, something to plug the gap until the rest of the steel fence had been repaired. Lisa knew that the speeding Audi, were it to divert towards that makeshift blockade, would go straight through the fence and drop into the Clyde.

Her blood ran cold. The cigarette fell from her mouth as she waited for the inevitable disaster.

The car hit the kerb, left the road and raced onto the path. There was one last sudden jerk but it wasn't enough for it to avoid the metal fencing. Then it was in the air. For a moment, the Audi looked like it was performing a stunt in a Hollywood movie. It hung there, defying the laws of physics.

A thudding splash. Sounded like a whale doing a belly flop.

The car was in the water.

Lisa watched in horror, paralysed by shock. After a moment, she was able to hurry over to the barrier.

The car floated for a while. Lisa could still hear a man's voice yelling from inside. Sounded like one word repeated over and over. What was he saying? A name? Then the Audi tipped forward, leaning heavily onto its front.

It was submerging.

"Roll the window down!" Lisa yelled, cupping her hands over her mouth. "Break the window."

Lisa knew that some people kept hammers in their car to break the glass in case of emergency. Even without a hammer, they could still pull the headrest off the seat and use the metal prods to shatter the glass. But Lisa couldn't hear the sound of breaking glass from down there on the surface of the water. Whoever was inside didn't have the luxury of a clear mind. They were panicking.

The Audi was going under fast. The passengers were still inside.

"Holy shit!" Lisa said, her heart racing. She looked around to see if anyone else was coming. Surely, someone else had seen this. Heard the sound of the car hitting the water. But there was no one, not a single soul in sight. The tower block and the houses behind Lisa were silent.

She leaned further over the barrier, looking down into the muddy brown water of the Clyde. The view inspired a surge of adrenaline. You're going in there, she thought. There was no way she couldn't do it. No way she could live with herself if she didn't at least try to save those people. Lisa was a strong swimmer who'd competed in numerous amateur competitions back in her teens and early twenties. Back when she'd been lean and strong. She still swam recreationally but there was no doubt she was a different person. She was plumper, softer. Both in body and mind.

Was she really going to do this?

Another glance over her shoulder. The sound of wailing sirens was absent. There was only the silence that followed the crash, a vacuum of noise that was both banal and chilling.

Lisa was on her own.

She kicked off her shoes, climbed over the barrier and positioned herself at the edge of the wall. She took several deep breaths, filling her lungs with air. Then she dove into the water.

Lisa hit the surface with a loud crash. The impact felt like an explosion going off inside her body. Now she was under, kicking, trying to get her bearings. The cold was sudden but not as bad as she'd anticipated. Visibility was okay. There was a greenish hue to the murky water and brown and green fragments floating around like a tiny alien race living peacefully under the surface.

She saw a froth up ahead. Lisa swam halfway towards it, then came back up for another gulp of air. There was still no one at the river's edge. Lisa figured the inhabitants of the tower block must have heard the sound of screeching tyres and raised voices all the time and put it down to boy racers, teenage drivers zooming around the riverside roads for kicks.

"Help!" Lisa yelled. Her voice, a flimsy squawk, didn't travel. "Help."

She swam front crawl towards the froth where the car hit the surface. Lisa filled her lungs one last time and down she went. Everything below the surface sounded muffled, loud and close all at the same time. She dove deeper into that other world, kicking as hard as she could.

There it was, up ahead.

The white Audi was fully submerged, still tilting where the weight of the engine was pulling it down into the river. Lisa had no idea how deep the Clyde was here or how fast a car like that would sink. She kicked furiously, navigating her way towards the passenger side window.

The back of a man's head was pressed up at the window. Blond hair. Curly hair, the strands dancing underwater.

Lisa hesitated, wondering at first if she was looking at a dead body. Then she thumped the glass with a hammer-like fist. There was no response so she tried again. The man in the passenger seat spun around. His face leapt out at Lisa, whose heart almost stopped.

It was Tommy.

Her husband was in the car drowning.

Lisa recoiled in horror, as if some foul underwater beast had pounced at her face. Tommy, despite the deep shit he was already in, looked just as horrified to see Lisa outside the window, swimming in the river. His eyes were bulbous, swelling up with panic. He shook his head like he was trying to knock it off his shoulders. Lisa couldn't imagine what he must have been thinking. Maybe Tommy thought he was dead. Maybe it was a shared nightmare.

A white metallic Audi. Of course, Lisa thought. This was Tommy's car. But what was he doing in the passenger seat?

She glanced beyond her husband to the young woman

sitting slumped forward at the wheel, motionless. The woman looked lifeless, like a pretty mannequin twisted into a slouch. Lisa recognised the driver. It was like a cold knife to the heart. Abbey Donaldson was a familiar face around the Kelvindale area and had been for a year and a half. She was a twenty-year-old student living in a flatshare with three other girls, just a few streets along from where the Grangers lived.

Lisa's arms and legs seized up. She began to sink along with the car before she remembered to kick.

Abbey Donaldson, she thought. So that's who you decided to go with this time Tommy. Gorgeous little Abbey. Slim and vivacious.

The tendons in Lisa's arms and legs pulled tight like rope.

Abbey originally came from a nearby traveller community but had at some point, broken away from her family's alternative lifestyle to attend college in the city centre. She was pretty in the classic sense: slim, tall and blonde. Not much in the way of curves but Tommy had always liked his women long and lean. The way Lisa used to be. Lisa considered Abbey to be a flirt, often seen out and about in the local pubs flirting disgracefully with older men. She seemed intent on finding herself a sugar daddy every night of the week. Maybe it was just her nature, Lisa wasn't sure. Since moving to the area, Abbey had taken to saying hi to both Tommy and Lisa as if they knew each other. Lisa was wary. Tommy on the other hand, always tried to be polite. That was Tommy – he always had a smile and a wave for everyone. Lisa had thought little more of it.

Abbey's eyes were closed. Lisa didn't know if the girl was unconscious or dead. A cloud of red mist seeped out of a horrendous-looking gash in her forehead. Lisa noticed that she hadn't been wearing her seatbelt. The airbags in Tommy's car hadn't deployed either. Defective sensors? Something about the nature of the drop that hadn't triggered them?

An empty crisp packet, along with some papers and a plastic Coke bottle, floated around the back of the car. The window behind the driver's seat was partially open. Some of the rubbish spilled slowly through the gap.

All these observations passed through Lisa's mind in a matter of seconds. She felt like an egg that had been cracked open. Yes, she'd suspected Tommy was cheating but Abbey's name had never crossed Lisa's mind for one second. She was twenty for God's sake and yet it was so obvious now that Lisa thought about it. Those little greetings they'd exchanged on the street. The friendliness, so informal as if they'd known each other for years. Lisa felt the crushing weight of humiliation pushing her down towards the river bed. Tommy was thirty-nine years old. He liked younger women and Lisa had always known it. His first affair, which lasted three months, had been with Laura Stevenson, a local dental assistant who was twelve years his junior.

Long, slim and pretty. Just like Abbey.

I'll never do it again, he'd promised Lisa. There'd been weeks and months of talking. Of couples counselling. Of marital reconstruction.

Now he'd done it again. He'd humiliated Lisa by copping off with a younger model, a prettier model, and all for what? To cling onto the pretence of youth? To fuel his vanity by yielding to the old urges, finding out if he still had it? Lisa had eventually forgiven him for Laura Stevenson. It hadn't been easy but she'd swallowed the pain and taken him back into their house. But hadn't she always feared deep down that Tommy would do it again? Hadn't she always known?

She was in a trance. Holding her breath. Waiting for the darkness to seep in and take it all away.

The loud thumping dragged her back to the present. Tommy was slamming his fists off the window. Slamming his elbows against the glass. What Tommy seemed to have forgotten in his panic was that the passenger side door would open now that the car was fully underwater. Lisa knew that vehicle doors were only jammed shut as long as the car was sinking, as the rising water pushed up against it. That tended to dishearten people who, after trying and failing to get out, thought of the doors as a lost cause.

Lisa stared at him. Tommy needed help. Tommy was dying and his brain, starved of oxygen, was betraying him, keeping him trapped in a state of primal terror where all he could do was hit the glass and hope for the best.

She reached for the door handle. There was still time to help him. To get Tommy out and maybe together they'd have enough strength to kick their way back to the surface. It was too late for Abbey. But saving one out of two was still very much on the cards.

Save him, she told herself. You *have* to save him. He's your husband for God's sake.

Lisa felt like she was floating in outer space. Weightless, far removed from the world of the everyday. Tommy made a weird gargling noise from inside the submerged car. His face was morphing into a grotesque Halloween mask version of itself, one frozen in an expression of suffocating terror.

She kicked away from the door.

You had your second chance.

The anger fuelled Lisa's retreat from the Audi. Let him drown side by side with his slut. Let their metal coffin sink all the way to the bottom of the river and beyond. How could he? After all they'd been through together as a couple.

After all they'd survived. The fertility treatment, the miscarriage, the death of Lisa's parents in a car crash seven years ago. It had always been Lisa and Tommy against the world and despite the many road bumps along the way, they'd always made it. They were supposed to be a team.

Look at him, Lisa thought. He looks so helpless.

She'd made her decision. As she kicked towards the surface the noise began to fade leaving only a cold, underwater silence. Tommy's thumping was a faint tapping. His sluggish limbs had run out of juice.

Down here, Lisa thought, it's a different world. There was no sense of law. No right or wrong. No crime, no punishment. Not like up there in the land of the shimmering grey sky where people would judge her for leaving her husband to die. The world beneath the surface was different. Down here, justice was instant.

Lisa looked back. She saw the darkening outline of the car, its distinctive contours merging with the river.

She kicked hard and cut through the surface, gasping for air. Any longer down there and she would've drowned too. But what was that noise? Lisa heard what sounded like a car pulling up at the side of the river. Voices, getting closer. Yelling and screaming.

At last, people were coming.

She took another massive gulp of air and went under.

Lisa swam, her stroke fluid and graceful. She felt light and free and capable of swimming like a mermaid, as she'd done in her youth. She put plenty of distance between herself and the car, trying to outrace the chilling silence that followed her. No thumping of hands and elbows off the glass. Not anymore. The sight of Tommy's eyes ballooning to the size of footballs was gone.

But what if they get him out? Lisa tightened up at the

thought. What if they got to him in time? It would be a miracle but it was still possible that a first-aider might be able to revive him, right?

No, Lisa thought. Tommy was dead.

She surfaced, filling her lungs with oxygen. The panicked yelling of onlookers was further downriver and this was Lisa's chance to escape the water unseen. She front crawled to the edge and pulled herself up onto the grassy bank. Lisa was breathing hard and yet she felt calm despite what had just happened. How was she supposed to get home like this? Dripping wet. Shaking like a leaf. She had a spare key to Deb's flat and that was her best shot. Could she do it? Get back there, wait for Deb to go to work and then sneak in and borrow some clothes? Then she'd get an Uber back to the house.

The empty house.

Lisa hurried up the grassy bank, stumbling her way onto the footpath. She was on the opposite side of the river now from where she'd started. There was no time to lose. She walked, her body starting to stiffen like a board. She felt her stomach clench up. That brief moment of calm she'd felt was gone. It was the thought of going home. Walking through the front door. Seeing the house as it had been. The framed photographs on the wall. All the reminders of Tommy sprinkled everywhere in every particle of the building. He *was* that house, as much as she was.

"Tommy," she whispered.

Lisa staggered onto the soft grass, almost falling over. Then she did fall. She dropped onto her hands and knees, managing to crawl a few metres before throwing up.

ONE YEAR LATER

3

Lisa opened her eyes and saw a shimmering beam of golden-white light. An intruder. It had sneaked through a gap in the curtains and ruined the perfect gloom of her bedroom in the morning. That was it then. One of Lisa's rare, dreamless sleeps had ended abruptly.

She turned onto her side, shielding her eyes from the light. Hoping that sleep would take her back into the void.

The sheets were soaked in sweat again. The nightmares had been growing more vivid over the past few weeks and of course, it was the anniversary of Tommy's death stirring things up. The date had been looming for so long and now here it was. Twelve months to the day since the Audi had gone into the river.

There'd be more rough nights to come, long after the anniversary was over. This thing wasn't going anywhere.

She sat up in bed, her Ramones t-shirt glued to her skin. It felt like climbing out of the river all over again.

With an exhausted groan, Lisa peeled the damp sheets off her legs. She leaned forward, drank some water from a glass on the bedside table. Lisa always left water by the bed these days. The amount of sweating she was doing, rehydration was the first priority of the day.

All she wanted to do was pull the sheets over her head. Stay buried there until the day was over.

Tommy's one-year memorial had been scheduled for months. That meant Lisa *had* to get up. She had to function, show face to Tommy's family and play the part of the grieving widow, still grieving after a year but doing her best to get on with things. Lisa had deliberately kept Tommy's mother, Iris, along with his two elder sisters, at bay for the past twelve months. It wasn't easy and if she had to see them, meetings were kept brief. Lisa had rejected all offers of help, taking on the role of the strong, independent woman.

Today, she couldn't avoid being around them. Nothing short of a fatal heart attack would excuse her from the gathering.

Lisa glanced up at the ceiling, at the cracked white plasterboard. She closed her eyes, ground her teeth together. A full day of Tommy worshipping, that's what awaited her in Victoria Park. That's what she feared most of all. The family were going to turn Tommy the cheat into Tommy the saint and everyone else was supposed to play along and pretend that the youngest of the Granger siblings wasn't a two-timing scumbag who'd played Lisa for a fool.

It was bullshit. But she had to be there.

Lisa grabbed the cigarette pack off the table and flipped the lid open. Using her teeth, she pulled one out the pack and lit up. That was one good thing about living alone, she thought, blowing a cloud of smoke across the bedroom and watching it disperse. The freedom to smoke whenever she wanted. Sure, the house reeked like a giant ashtray but it complimented the smell of alcohol, the other consistent odour under Lisa's roof since Tommy's death.

She pushed herself off the bed, walked over to the full-length mirror. Lisa stepped over the cardboard boxes, paper bags and empty food wrappers lying around everywhere. She stared at her reflection. She'd lost weight over the past year and not in a healthy eating, go to the gym kind of way. God, she was hollow and sunken around the face. Cheekbones to die for. Almost forty-years-old and modelling the heroin chic look that had rocked back in the nineties.

Murderer.

The voice whispered the same accusation every day. Several times a day. It was always Tommy's voice that uttered the word.

Shit, Lisa thought.

What would they say to her? All the sympathetic faces gathered in Victoria Park today. *Oh, you look great Lisa*. And all the while, their eyes would look up and down in horror, wondering where all the weight went. You don't smile anymore Lisa, they'd say. But that's all they'd say. They wouldn't say anything about the accident or about who'd been in the car with Tommy that day and what it meant for Tommy the saint's reputation. No one ever talked about that.

The police had found nothing wrong with the Audi after hauling it out of the river. The brakes worked. There were no other mechanical failures to report and the car was in outstanding condition, no surprise to Lisa because she knew that Tommy took good care of the Audi, his pride and joy. The two deaths were attributed to human error or human something or other. Suicide pact? A heated argument gone wrong? That was the media talking and Tommy's family paid no attention to the media. They didn't pay attention several days later when it was announced that Abbey had been nine weeks pregnant.

Made sense, Lisa thought. Tommy had plucked out a young fertile woman from the crowd, pretty and energetic, someone who could give him the son he so badly wanted. Lisa never stood a chance. Not while Abbey had the ability to make Tommy a father.

She'd tried to pick up the pieces in the days and weeks that followed the crash. To get back to a so-called normal life, whatever that was. Lisa went back to work as a GP vet, working in a nice little clinic which she'd co-founded with her partner, Malcolm, in the west end. The work was a godsend. For a while, Lisa had been all over the long hours. Sleep, eat, work. Repeat. It kept her mind off things, at least for a while.

Lisa took a step back from the mirror, the cigarette still hanging from her lips. She laughed. Tommy would go apeshit if he could see how messy the house was. She could almost feel his disapproval, like he was still there in the house. But Tommy *was* there. He was in the walls, in the floor, in the ceiling and in the cracks in the ceiling too. The scent of his aftershave was still potent, usually late at night when Lisa was in the bathroom getting ready for bed. She'd tried to put him away. To bury him all over again by putting his things away. All the photos of Tommy were hidden in a cardboard storage box, tucked away at the bottom of the wardrobe and buried under a pile of shoes. On the rare occasion that someone came over, Lisa would put a few of the better pictures out. Afterwards, they were straight back in the box.

She pulled the bedroom curtains open, wincing at the daylight. Opening the window, Lisa leaned outside and inhaled fresh air with a hint of fumes and chemicals. She glanced skyward, hoping to see rainclouds. There was only a neverending sheet of blue and a bright sun. Lisa sighed. No chance of the weather calling a halt to proceedings.

"You're going," she said. "Deal with it."

What bugged Lisa the most about Tommy's family (and there were many things) was their blind refusal to accept the obvious – that their son had been cheating on his wife. The Grangers were delusional. They paid no attention to the obvious and instead, led by Iris, they continued to parrot the line that Tommy the angel had been giving the poor wee girl a lift and that something had gone wrong. Maybe Tommy had a heart attack or *something*. It was some kind of health issue and Abbey had taken the wheel to drive him to hospital and unable to handle the car and in a full-blown panic, she'd driven them into the Clyde. Lisa couldn't believe the mental gymnastics. They'd ignored the brief media speculation. The local gossip about adultery and suicide pacts. Tommy was a good boy. There was no way it was anything other than a terrible accident.

The Grangers didn't know about Tommy's first affair with Laura Stevenson. Lisa didn't see the point in bringing it up now, even though she wanted to. What good would bursting their bubble do?

They'd be out in force today. All his family and friends. His control freak of a mother, his two elder sisters, his eighty-nine-year-old gran who now carried an adorable childhood picture of Tommy in a locket around her neck. His nephew, Ewan, who'd idolised his uncle, would be there. And all the rest of them. His work colleagues too.

So many of them.

Lisa sometimes got a bad feeling. She felt like the Grangers knew what really happened. What she'd done that day, turning her back on their golden boy and letting him die. As she lay in bed late at night, this would haunt her. It was hard to explain, but she couldn't shake it off. It was a subtle feeling. Sometimes she believed the family members were waiting for the right occasion to expose her. To bring justice to Tommy.

The one-year memorial. Wouldn't that be the perfect time to strike?

It was a silly thought, Lisa said to herself.

It was ridiculous.

She trudged downstairs and ate a light breakfast of toast and coffee. Afterwards, Lisa hopped in the shower. She picked out a light floral summer dress that she'd bought for the occasion two weeks ago. Only the best for Tommy. It's a celebration, Iris had told her. A celebration of Tommy's wonderful life on this planet. Don't wear black. He wouldn't have wanted us to wear black.

"Fuck you Tommy," Lisa said, once she was back in front of the mirror. She glanced at the quarter bottle of Glen's vodka beside the bed.

Just a sip, she thought.

4

Lisa walked through the underpass that led to Victoria park's southern entrance.

Often labelled as one of Glasgow's prettiest parks, Victoria Park drew many visitors to its Fossil Grove, which housed the remnants of an ancient forest, fossilised tree stumps estimated at around three hundred and thirty million years old. As well as a boating pond, it boasted an extensive range of floral displays, carpet bedding and hollies. There were paths running around the flowerbeds for easy pedestrian access. For those who wanted to take the weight off their feet and enjoy the view, wooden benches were scattered at regular intervals.

Tommy had grown up in the shadow of the park. He'd always kept fond memories of the place and he and Lisa had gone for frequent walks there, at least at the beginning of their relationship.

The memorial was set up around the flower displays. Lisa walked over that way, greeting a few familiar faces in between grabbing a glass of red wine off the drinks table. Sipping the wine, she had a good look around. It was as she'd expected. The memorial was a shrine to Tommy Granger and it wasn't even trying to be anything else. Iris had left no stone unturned when it came to honouring her boy's memory. There were massive concert-sized speakers dotted around the gardens, melancholic piano instrumentals trickling out of each one. Everybody was dressed in bright, summery colours as Iris had requested. Some wore Hawaiian shirts so bright that sunglasses were required to look at them. There were tables and chairs scattered around, some for sitting, others for holding the drinks, sandwiches and other nibbles.

Two large screens had been erected on opposite ends of the floral gardens. Both played a neatly edited montage of home movie footage taken from the Granger family archives.

"Oh shit," Lisa said.

The grainy clips showed Tommy at various stages of his short life. He was a wild-haired boy chasing a football in a caravan park. His two sisters, tall, blonde and dressed in matching shorts and t-shirts, chased after their overexcited brother who squealed with excitement and lost control of the ball as the chase intensified. Cut to a series of childhood birthdays. The angelic blond child blowing out the candles, tearing open presents but not once forgetting to smile at the camera and thank his mummy for the wonderful gifts. The look of pure joy on his face when he walked in on his first bike on Christmas morning – a BMX Falcon Pro. The second screen played clips of the older Tommy. Tommy's graduation day. He was so gangly and awkward, not quite as filled out or handsome as he'd become in his twenties. Tommy on holiday, lying on a sunbed beside the swimming pool. Flexing his muscles for the camera. Tommy learning to drive. Tommy at the gym, grim and serious as he lifted weights. Tommy getting married and there was Lisa in those clips, the young, fresh-faced version of herself in the beautiful wedding dress that still hung in Iris's wardrobe.

So much footage. It was as if someone had been following Tommy around with a camera for his entire life. Preparing for a documentary.

Lisa turned away. What next? Would either one of the screens show Tommy trapped in the car under the Clyde? His face distorted. Hitting the glass with his fists and elbows. Saying 'Lisa' over and over in a gargled, drowning voice.

You're here, Lisa thought. She could feel it. Tommy was in the park, a shadowy figure standing on the outskirts. There he was, in between the gaps in the trees by the outer fencing. He was sitting on every park bench watching her.

Lisa picked up a second glass of wine. Did her best to mingle, reminding herself that it was nearly over.

She spoke to the family. To the mother, sisters, nephew and to Tommy's old gran, Isobel, who was wheelchair bound and overjoyed to see Lisa after a long absence. Lisa tried to act in an appropriate manner around these people. She regretted not moving away from Glasgow earlier, avoiding the situation of being so close to Tommy's family. She couldn't breathe when they were around. She'd played the grieving widow for a year, processing Tommy's absence and also trying to come to terms with the choice she'd made that day in the water. Some days it felt like she'd done the right thing. There was barely a twinge of guilt. On other days, she felt like a cold-blooded murderer and couldn't leave the house. In the days and weeks that followed Tommy's death, Lisa had jumped out of her skin every time the doorbell rang or she heard voices outside on the street. Lisa was convinced that the world would know the truth soon enough. And then? All the sympathy she'd received would turn to horror. Someone would creep up behind her. She'd feel a hand on her shoulder, pushing her down. Someone in a suit and tie with a badge, wearing a sombre expression, would say, 'We know what you did.'

Lisa wanted to tell them about Tommy. She wanted to walk around the flower gardens with a microphone, her voice blasting out of those big speakers as she told the guests about the serial adulterer who'd taken her for a fool.

"Poor wee lassie," they'd say about Abbey. "He must have been giving her a lift. Something must have happened."

Heart attack. Stroke. A blinding light on the road to Damascus. Anything, so long as it wasn't an affair.

Lisa needed space. She drank her wine and took a third glass over to one of the benches. She didn't look at the big screen on her way. She didn't need to see Tommy as a cute child anymore. His blond hair, white and puffed out like a giant ball of candy floss. That adorable smile.

She sat down for a minute before she became aware of someone standing over her. Lisa braced herself to play 'the widow' again, but when she looked up it was her friend, Risha, standing over her.

Her friend. Risha had nothing to do with the Grangers.

Thank God.

Risha Nawaz was a family doctor working out of a well-respected medical practice on Dumbarton Road. She and her family had spent the first three years of her life in Pakistan, then a year in Uganda, before her family eventually settled in Scotland. It was in a nearby primary school, just a mile east of Victoria Park, that she'd met Lisa and Deb. The three girls bonded quickly and had been close ever since, staying in touch through university and beyond.

"Hey you," Risha said, smiling. She was dressed in a two-piece summer outfit, brown and gold, with an Eastern flavour. Her long black hair, almost always tied back, hung loose over her shoulders.

"Hey," Lisa said, standing up and embracing her old friend. "You look great."

Risha's eyes gave Lisa's skinny frame the once-over. "You too. Love the dress."

"Thanks," Lisa said, sitting back down.

"So how's it going?" Risha asked, joining Lisa on the bench. She spoke with a soft Glaswegian accent but there was still a hint of the exotic in her voice. "Haven't seen you in ages."

Lisa shrugged. "It's alright. I could do without this memorial."

"That good, eh?"

"Yep."

"What's wrong? Or is that a stupid question?"

Lisa took a hurried sip of wine. She glanced at Risha and frowned. "You don't have a drink?"

"Bit early in the day for me," Risha said with an embarrassed smile. "I had a couple of glasses last night and even that's rare for me nowadays."

Lisa shook her head. "What the hell happened to us?"

"We got old and boring."

"We used to put vodka away like it was lemonade," Lisa said. "Painting the town red every weekend. Then you'd wake up in the morning, not a hint of a headache. I want to be that person again. I didn't appreciate her enough."

A cool breeze blew across the park. Lisa pulled the hem of her dress further down her legs.

Risha nodded towards one of the big TV screens. "Iris going a little overboard, is she?"

Lisa leaned her elbow on top of the bench. She couldn't

seem to get comfortable. "You know what bugs the shit out of me?"

"What?"

"She never asked, you know? Iris never asked if I wanted any of this. Of...*this*. Didn't even think to ask if I wanted a memorial. They just expect me to stand here and be an ornament."

Risha sighed. "Did you know they're having a memorial for Abbey today too?"

Lisa felt her joints tensing up. That name was all it took to make her squirm in her seat. "Careful you don't say her name too loudly. I don't think Iris and the Granger gang could handle it."

She looked at Risha.

"How do you know they're having a memorial?"

"There's a Facebook page dedicated to her memory. I follow it."

"You follow it? Why?"

"Why not? I followed everything about the accident at first, just to keep in the loop. They don't post much but there was one about her memorial last week. Doesn't bother you, does it?"

Lisa gave a half-hearted shrug. She could hear the sound of bees buzzing in the flower gardens. "Where is it?"

"Southside. In a pub."

Lisa nodded. "I bet you it's a better party than this one. Can't see the travellers trying to turn Abbey into a saint. Can you?"

"Oh Lisa," Risha said, sitting forward and taking in the sights of the memorial. "This is...*nice*. Tommy was loved, there's no denying that. The old home movie footage is incredible. That must have taken some effort to splice together, no?"

Lisa chewed on her bottom lip. "Wouldn't know. I wasn't asked, remember?"

"Of course," Risha said. "Different people mourn in different ways. And I know Tommy was no angel."

Lisa tried to smile. Couldn't quite pull it off. Risha was one of the few people in Lisa's inner circle who knew about Tommy's first affair with the young dental assistant. And although they'd never talked explicitly about Abbey, Risha was too smart to swallow the bullshit narrative about Tommy giving her a lift and having some kind of episode behind the wheel.

"Nobody's talking about Abbey," Lisa said. "You notice that? You heard anyone mention her name around here?"

Risha shrugged. "I just got here."

"I've got no love for the girl," Lisa said. "But she was pregnant. She died, the baby died and yet it's Tommy this, Tommy that."

"Well, I suppose it's *his* memorial."

Lisa glared at the gathering in front of her.

"I'm sorry Lisa," Risha said, inching closer on the bench. "Why didn't you say anything to me at the time? You must have had your suspicions that Tommy was up to no good again."

"I wasn't a hundred percent sure."

Risha lowered her voice. "The papers said Abbey had a boyfriend at the time. Remember? Her flatmates agreed but said that Abbey never brought him back to the flat. So, you know, maybe it wasn't Tommy who got her..."

Lisa held up a hand.

"Tommy *was* the boyfriend they're talking about. The reason she didn't bring him back to the flat was because he was a married man and her flatmates would've known that.

They would have seen Tommy around. Me too. And as much as I want to believe the baby wasn't his..."

She shook her head.

"I know," Risha said.

Lisa stared at the diminutive figure of Iris Granger, holding court with a small group of people beside the pond. Iris must have known, deep down that she'd given birth to two Tommys. There was the real Tommy and then there was Tommy the archangel who could do no wrong. And for the rest of her days, Iris would cultivate the myth of the archangel son. She would cling to it, make it real by wishing alone. Meanwhile, the real Tommy's corpse was rotting in a cemetery in the southside of Glasgow.

"I feel sorry for her," Risha said.

"For who?"

"Abbey."

Lisa threw her friend a furious look "Why? That wee slut knew Tommy was married when she went after him. And yes, I'm certain *she* was the pursuer. She even had the gall to say hello to me in the street."

"I know," Risha said, hands up in surrender pose. "I just meant that it was terrible the way she was overlooked in the news reports at the time. They barely mentioned her and she's only a kid really."

"My heart bleeds for her."

"Whatever else she'd done," Risha said, "she didn't deserve to die like that. The baby certainly didn't."

"I don't want to talk about Abbey Donaldson anymore," Lisa said. "What's done is done. And it wasn't a baby – it was only about the size of a cherry."

They sat in silence, watching the dogwalkers who frequented the park, all of them keeping a respectful distance from the memorial. Lisa wondered if Iris had sought out formal permission to use this section of the park. Or had she just barged in and done her thing? Wouldn't surprise Lisa if it was the latter.

A set of heavy, plodding footsteps approached the bench.

"Auntie Lisa?"

Lisa looked up. Ewan Granger, Tommy's twenty-one-year-old nephew, was standing over her. Ewan was the only child of Sheila McKenzie, Tommy's oldest sister. Ewan and Tommy had been close. More like best friends than uncle and nephew. The absence of a father figure from an early age had drawn Ewan closer to Tommy as he'd grown up. He was a shy, awkward lad. Big and good-looking with a deep voice, but a little lacking in the brains department. He had the signature blond curls although today he'd covered them up under an LA Dodgers beanie.

Ewan, along with Granny Isobel, was one of the few Grangers that Lisa liked. Unlike the others, they didn't look at her with an expression of thinly-veiled disappointment as if she'd failed Tommy. As if she'd failed *them*.

"How's it going Ewan?" she asked, standing up and giving the lad a brief hug. She felt a stab of guilt whenever she looked at the poor guy. After all, she was the reason that Ewan didn't have a father figure in his life anymore.

"Aye," he said with a bored shrug. "I'm alright."

Lisa gestured to the people, the screens and the pretty flower gardens that surrounded them. "Nice here. Isn't it?"

His voice was a colourless rumble.

"It's alright."

Ewan glanced at Risha, then back at Lisa. His hands were thrust deep in his pockets. "Want me to get some drinks?"

Lisa held her glass up. "I'm good, thanks."

"I'm fine too," Risha added. "I'll get something in a while. Thanks though."

Lisa gave Ewan's arm a gentle squeeze. "So how are you *really* doing Ewan? No bullshit pal. You don't have to pretend."

Another shrug of those wide shoulders. "Just miss him. You know?"

Lisa nodded. "Me too."

"I've not seen you much at my granny's house," Ewan said. "You not coming round for Sunday lunch anymore?"

Lisa shook her head, a visual apology and a weak one at that. "I've been busy. Working weekends, you know? It helps keep my mind occupied. I do miss those lunches though. Does your mum still go?"

"Aye. Everyone but you."

"I'll try Ewan. See how it goes."

"Aye. It's cool."

"What are you up to anyway? Still in college?"

"Nah, I left. Wasn't for me – it was just like school, eh? Doing an electrician apprenticeship now with Jim Starkey."

Lisa had no idea who Jim Starkey was. "Good for you. You enjoying it?"

He shrugged. "It's alright."

Sheila Granger, her sister Kelly, and their mother Iris, appeared at Ewan's shoulder. The Three Witches, Lisa thought. She watched as the tall, Amazonian figure of Sheila draped her arm around her son. She gave him a tight squeeze.

"Ma wee boy hassling you Lisa darling?"

Lisa smiled at Ewan. "Nah. He's good."

Sheila kissed her son hard on the cheek. Ewan's face wrinkled in protest. At that moment, he seemed to regress to a ten-year-old boy, embarrassed in his mother's presence.

He glanced at Risha, hoping she wasn't paying attention to his mother's demonstrative display of affection.

"We're going to put some flowers on the pond in a few minutes," Sheila said, turning her attention back to Lisa. "Mum's going to say a few words. Bit of poetry, eh? You coming?"

Lisa's insides clenched up at the thought.

"Okay."

Both of Iris's daughters wore blinding, multi-coloured summer dresses that looked too tacky for a Hawaiian tourist beach. Their skin, as usual, was plastered in fake tan, their faces buried under layers of thick makeup. Sheila was a big woman with strong swimmer-like arms, cultivated over hours in the gym and in the local pool. She was a runner too, regularly participating in marathons for charity. Kelly was tall and slimmer than her sister, more conventionally pretty. If there was a quiet one in the family, it was her.

Iris stepped forward, filling the narrow gap in between her two surviving children. The girls dwarfed their mother. Now in her late sixties, Iris was still a sprightly woman with short dyed brown hair and a formidable expression.

"Would you like to say something Lisa?" she asked. "You are his wife after all."

Lisa glanced at Risha. She took a deep breath. "Nah, I'd only screw it up. I'm hopeless at that kind of thing."

"Okay sweetheart. That's fine."

Lisa didn't like the way the three Granger women were looking at her. She'd never liked the way they looked at her but what was that she saw in their eyes? What were they expecting from Lisa?

A confession?

Was today the day after all?

"Five minutes," Sheila said, threading her arm through

Iris's and leading her mum back towards the floral displays. "We'll see you both by the water, eh?"

Lisa's response was a feeble nod of the head. She watched as mother, daughters and Ewan went on their way, rounding up the other guests and steering them towards the pond.

Three wolves, Lisa thought, herding the sheep.

"This'll be fun," Risha said in a dry voice, standing up alongside Lisa. "Shall we go over?"

Lisa put her wine glass on the bench. A sudden light-headedness had come over her. What if Iris, Sheila and Kelly were baiting her and the upcoming speech by Iris wasn't a tribute to Tommy after all, but instead the moment of the big reveal? When they outed her as Tommy's killer. What then? The Grangers and their extended mob would sprout fangs and...

"Lisa?"

She felt Risha tapping her on the shoulder.

"What?"

"You okay? You're zoning out sweetheart. Look, I hope you don't mind me saying Lisa, but I can't help notice that you've lost a lot of weight. Maybe a little too much, don't you think?"

Lisa turned to her friend. "I can't be here right now. I need to go. This...this isn't good for me."

"Too much wine?"

"There's somewhere I have to go," Lisa said, wrapping her arms around Risha before backing off.

Risha blinked hard. Pointed over to the pond. "What about the speech?"

"You're right," Lisa said. "Everyone mourns differently. This might be okay for them but I need something else. I need to do something for me."

"Do you want me to come with you?" Risha asked.

"No. I have to go by myself."

Lisa backpedalled towards the foot of a winding path that spiralled upwards. The path led to the Broomhill exit on the other side of the park.

Her eyes were locked on the other guests. She was terrified that one of them would see her trying to leave early.

"What about Iris?" Risha asked. "What am I supposed to say to her?"

"Tell her I'm not feeling well. You're a doctor. Come up with some medical jargon that will confuse the shit out of her, okay?"

"Is that true?" Risha asked. "*Are* you unwell?"

"I'll be fine once I get out of here."

Risha nodded. "Okay, I'll make something up. And I'll do my best to make it look convincing."

Lisa managed a weak smile. "Thanks Risha." She started towards the winding path, barely hearing Risha's voice creeping up behind her.

"And pick up the phone when I call you, okay? At least answer a text once in a while. Lisa. Do you hear me?"

Lisa heard. But she didn't answer.

5

The journey to Cathcart Cemetery took twenty minutes.

Lisa thanked the Uber driver and stepped out of the car, still a little tipsy after the wine she'd consumed at the memorial. Considering she'd only picked at her breakfast that morning, she'd been drinking on an empty stomach. Again. It was a beautiful afternoon in the southside with clear skies and the gentle breeze whispering back and forth touched Lisa's face like a caress. The surrounding foliage swayed percussively.

Going to the memorial had been a mistake. She'd always known it would be but the experience itself had been worse than she'd imagined. It was a sham. One big lie. All this Tommy the saint shit was messing with her head.

Lisa had come to Cathcart to see the real Tommy.

She crossed the narrow road, stopping at the cemetery gate to light a cigarette. God, she was starting to crave them now. There'd been no intention to get hooked but didn't every smoker say the same thing? She smoked half the cigarette before stubbing it out under her foot. Then she walked through the gate and into the grounds.

Cathcart Cemetery, a forty-three-acre site, was named after the nearby neighbourhood of Cathcart. The cemetery was bounded to the east by the White Cart Water and Linn Park, situated on the opposite bank. It was divided into two parts, one section with the older, more historically appealing graves and the newer section where the modern burials took place. It was on Netherlee Road, amongst the recently deceased that Lisa walked now.

It was peaceful in there. A giant garden cemetery, the grounds bordered by a towering wall of trees to the south. It was the perfect place to stop and contemplate life, death and also to feel a little closer to nature. The grass was neat and tidy under Lisa's feet. There were no upturned headstones or any other signs of vandalism in the cemetery.

It was a short walk to Tommy's grave from the gate. Lisa hadn't been back here to visit since the six-month anniversary (an ordeal she'd been forced to endure with Iris and her tribe). Despite the length of time that had passed since her last visit, it was easy for her to find Tommy's grave.

She looked around. There was no one else in the cemetery.

Lisa took a right turn off the main path, walking onto a gravel track that ran in between two rows of headstones. After a few paces, she stopped.

"Hi Tommy."

The serif inscription on Tommy's granite headstone was every bit as unblemished as it had been a year ago. *Beloved son. Beloved brother. Beloved husband. Always in our hearts.*

A fresh bunch of flowers, pink and red carnations, had been propped up at the base of the slab. Most likely, Iris had been here earlier. The sisters too. Ewan, Granny Isobel, as well as some close family friends.

Lisa imagined it was disrespectful to smoke here, if not

illegal. And yet she couldn't help herself. She lit up in a hurry, inhaling deeply. Her trembling hand struggled to hold the cigarette.

"You should see what's happening at Victoria Park. They've got big screens with you all over them. They've got pretty flowers and food and drink and it's all for you Tommy my love. They're probably unveiling a life-sized statue of you as we speak. Boy, they loved you. They still love you."

Her voice cut through the soft breeze.

"And yet they didn't know you. Not like I did."

Lisa glanced over her shoulder, making sure she was still alone.

"I made a bad choice," she said, blowing smoke that was carried off in the gentle wind. "It was a terrible choice. I know that and I have to live with it. But we didn't have time to talk it through, did we? You said you'd never do it again. Then you knocked up a twenty-year-old and came home to me at night as everything was okay. Sitting beside me on the couch. Putting your hand on my leg, around my shoulder. Were you thinking about Abbey when you did that? Jesus, Tommy. You knocked her up. Do you have any idea how that makes me feel? I mean, do you have any clue?"

Lisa froze at the sight of a police car cruising along Netherlee road. This was a quiet little road where nothing happened. What were the police doing here? The car travelled slowly, unlike Lisa's heart which was going full throttle. The crazy thought that Iris Granger had sent the police to find her crossed Lisa's mind.

That was crazy, wasn't it?

The car drove past without stopping.

"Fuck."

Lisa was well aware of the paranoid nonsense running around her mind. It had been getting worse lately with the upcoming anniversary. But when it hit, it hit hard. And no matter how ludicrous the suggestion, she couldn't shake off the feeling that she was right. That the Grangers were out to get her. That they knew everything about what happened at the river.

"What did you tell her?" Lisa asked, turning back to Tommy's headstone. "Did you tell her you were going to marry her? Did you mean it?"

She dropped the cigarette butt. Kicked it at Tommy's slab.

"Would she have given you a boy, I wonder? You never said it back then. You know, back when the subject of children wasn't taboo. But I always knew you wanted a son."

She knelt down, picked up the flowers and checked their condition. Then she placed them at the base and straightened up.

"What happened to us?"

Lisa stood there, listening to the soft rustle of the trees.

"You're dead Tommy," she said. "Why can't you just stay dead?"

6

One week after the memorial, Lisa checked into a Premier Inn in Edinburgh's city centre.

She was in the capital for a three-day veterinary congress organised by the British Veterinary Association. The congress was scheduled to begin the next morning. As stated on the BVA website, the congress was designed to 'bring veterinary professionals together to debate and discuss the latest developments facing the profession.' Lisa was always keen to learn and grow as a vet but this particular trip to Edinburgh came at just the right time. She was glad to see the back of Glasgow for a few days.

No reminders of Tommy here.

After unpacking her bag in the hotel room, Lisa put the kettle on and collapsed onto the double bed. It was soft and comfortable enough to make her feel like she was drowning in the mattress. She waved her arms and legs as if making a snow angel. The relief of being in this room, far from anyone who knew her, was overwhelming. It was a pleasant enough space with its high-spec ensuite bathroom, smart

TV, sleek pull-out desk and excellent Wi-Fi. A trace of citrus air freshener lingered.

During the one-hour drive between Scotland's two major cities, Lisa had neglected the radio and podcast options. She'd been thinking about leaving Glasgow for good again. This trip, Lisa thought, was the perfect time to start making moves. Edinburgh was one possibility. Lisa had a soft spot for the capital and in between BVA sessions, she planned to do some research into local vet practices, maybe even pay some of them a visit in person. She had a few contacts too so it wouldn't mean the horror of cold calling. She'd also research areas to live. And there were other options too. England? Ireland? Wales? It was a lot work but she was looking forward to getting started.

For now, she had the evening to herself. The first sessions started tomorrow at nine o'clock and until then, Lisa could do whatever she wanted. The plan (as much as she'd formulated one) was to grab a bite to eat in the hotel, maybe do a little online networking and then watch a movie or read before sinking into a deep, uninterrupted eight-hour sleep.

No wine. One or two cigarettes at most.

Lisa sat up in bed, smiling and catching a glimpse of that smile in the mirror. She was still there, somewhere in that skeletal reflection. Something else she'd been considering was the prospect of dating again. Romance. Sex. It sounded alien to her after all this time and yet there it was, back on her mind. She longed for another body lying beside her in bed at night. To reach her arm out and touch something other than an unused pillow. Soon, she told herself. Once she'd settled into a new place, she'd get back in the mix. Maybe she'd use one of those dating apps. It was time to get out of her comfort zone.

But work and relocation were her priorities. Everything else came after that.

So much to think about.

Lisa's eyelids were closing over. She heard the kettle click from what seemed like miles away, letting her know that the water had boiled. She didn't get up. Lisa's head sank deeper into the soft, crisp pillow. Five minutes, she thought. That's all she needed. Then tea. Then she'd have a look at the menu.

It was going to be a good night. A productive night.

Just five minutes.

Lisa opened her eyes, blinking in confusion.

Her mobile phone was ringing but it might as well have been the four-minute warning signalling the start of nuclear war. Her arm shot out and she snatched the phone off the bedside table, thinking for a second that she was back in Kelvindale and that it was time to get up for work. Was Tommy up yet?

She sat up with a tired groan.

Hotel. Edinburgh. Conference. Nap.

Tommy was dead.

"Oh shit," Lisa mumbled in a tired, raspy voice. She glanced at the digital clock beside the bed and saw that it was past seven o'clock. Her five-minute nap had lasted two hours.

She looked at the phone. It was a private number calling. If this is a sales call, Lisa thought, I'm going to rip this person a new one. Who the hell makes a sales call at this time of night?

"Hello?"

No answer.

Lisa's second attempt was an impatient bark. She wasn't in the mood for technical hiccups or language barriers or anything for that matter except dismissing this call as abruptly as possible. "Hello?"

There was still no answer. She pulled the phone off her ear, glared at it and then hung up.

"Arsehole."

Lisa groaned again as she sat up further on the bed, pressing her back against the slat headrest. Why did she allow herself to fall asleep? She was supposed to be researching new places to live, to work, to be doing something productive with her time. Fat chance. It was so damn fuzzy in her head right now. She was already thinking about those eight-hours of sleep to come later.

Let's try again, she thought.

Tea. Start with tea.

Lisa got up to put the kettle on when the phone started ringing again. She felt a knot tighten in her gut but couldn't understand the sudden feeling of apprehension. There were dark whispers in her head, telling her that something awful was waiting on the other end of the line. It was stupid and Lisa knew it. Just the old paranoia flaring up again. She picked up the phone and answered in a firm voice.

"Hello?"

Silence.

"Hello?"

Lisa jammed her ear against the phone. The line wasn't dead – there *was* something there. A faint sound. Breathing.

"Who is this?"

Nothing.

She listened closely. This wasn't your typical heavy breather like in a creepy horror film. The blatant, over the top wheezing that was almost comical. There was nothing pervy or lewd about the sound in Lisa's ear. This was something else – it sounded like someone in difficulty. Someone with genuine respiratory problems. It was faint but it was there and it was slowly getting louder. The sound of someone gasping for air.

"Who is this?" Lisa asked, her voice still firm despite the surge of cold terror rising up inside her.

The voice was a whisper from afar.

"*I…*"

"What?" Lisa said. The aluminium iPhone case pressed to her ear felt like it was on fire. "Who is this?"

"*I…can't…breathe.*"

The phone slipped through Lisa's fingers. It fell onto the bed, landing on its back and the call duration display from 'Unknown' stared up at her, still ticking. Lisa stared back, wide-eyed as if she was looking at a bloody, decapitated head that she'd found under the covers.

She picked up the phone. Her arm was shaking.

"Please…"

"*Can't breathe Lisa.*"

Lisa could almost feel the caller's rancid breath tunnelling through her ear. She glanced at her reflection in the oval-shaped mirror across the room. At that moment, Lisa looked like the doomed victim in every slasher movie, shrunken to half her size, eyes bulging and staring into the eyes of the killer.

The fear gave birth to a bubbling anger. Lisa found her voice again and yelled into the mouthpiece.

"Who *is* this? Answer me."

She waited but the line was dead.

"Hello? Hello? Fuck!"

Lisa threw the phone down and jumped off the bed like

the sheets had caught fire. She ran across the room, pulled the door open and rushed into the hotel corridor. It was dead quiet. She looked both ways. There was nothing but a window at one end of the corridor and the beginnings of a staircase that led down to reception at the other. No people. All the doors were shut. Lisa strained her ears. She heard the sound of muffled voices and the tinny crackle of a TV spilling through the thin walls.

She backpedalled into her room. Quietly, as if retreating from a wild predator.

Lisa closed the door. She stood with her back shoved up against it, not certain if the danger was on the inside or outside. She immediately scolded herself. Danger, what danger? It was just a prank caller. Lisa walked over to the wardrobe and pulled the double doors open, just to check she was alone in the room. There was nothing in there, no monsters, no masked killers. Just the clothes she'd unpacked earlier and an ironing board.

She checked under the bed. Behind the curtains. It was stupid, childish even and she did it anyway.

The phone rang again. This time it was the landline on the bedside table and it was more of a stilted beep than the classic ringing sound of Lisa's iPhone. She walked towards the table, her legs like air. She picked up the handset, wary of putting her lips too close to the mouthpiece.

"Yes?"

"Mrs Granger?"

Lisa registered a young man's voice. Polite and formal.

"Speaking."

"This is reception calling. I'm sorry to disturb you but we've received a call for you and apparently, it's quite urgent. Is it okay to patch the call through to your room?"

"Who is it?" Lisa asked, looking at the door. It had a

deadbolt and security latch. Why the hell wasn't she using it? "Did they leave a name?"

"Yes they did."

"And?"

"It's Tommy."

The receptionist said it in such a matter-of-fact way that Lisa didn't react at first. After a moment, she wasn't even sure he'd said it at all. Most likely she'd imagined it because she was still sleepy after the unscheduled nap. Oh, it's Tommy. No big deal. No big deal that her dead husband was trying to get in touch with her via the reception of a Premier Inn.

"Mrs Granger? Are you still there?"

"Put him through."

"Thank you. Just a moment please."

Lisa had never experienced a silence like the one in between the receptionist's voice and whatever was coming next. A bead of sweat ran down her face. The phone was hot and damp against her ear.

A scratching noise.

"Is that you?" Lisa whispered.

About ten seconds passed in silence. Then a wet, raspy voice crawled out of the earpiece.

"Help me."

It was different but it *was* Tommy's voice.

"Who are you?"

"*Tommeeee.*"

Lisa thought of a child learning a new word. The syllables not fully stitched together yet.

"No, you're not Tommy. Please, tell me who you are and what you want."

"Tommeeee."

Lisa's rational mind was stubborn. It refused to accept

the bullshit ghost story running around her head. And yet that same story had been there long before she'd checked into the Premier Inn. It had been there for one year, the idea that Tommy was still alive. Somehow. But it was ridiculous to believe that her dead husband was talking to her on the phone. She'd visited his grave only a few days ago. Tommy was dead and this was someone else pretending to be him. That was all there was to it. Lisa wouldn't give them what they wanted. She wouldn't listen to the nagging, irrational voice that told her the impossible was possible.

"You're not Tommy," she said. Her frightened whisper was now an angry growl. "Who the fuck are you? How dare you do this to me? I can trace this call you know."

Lisa doubted very much that she'd be able to trace the call. Most likely, the caller, if they had at least half a brain, was using a prepaid throwaway phone. But she'd threaten them anyway. Maybe they were easy to scare off.

"*Tommeeee.*"

There was a faint crackling noise. Sounded like an old car radio, the dial stuck in between stations.

"Tommeeee."

Lisa almost pulled the phone cord out of the wall. "Tommy? Oh really? It's you is it? Are you willing to prove that?"

A pause.

"My nickname," Lisa said. "What was the nickname you called me? Huh, *sweetheart*? The first nickname, the only nickname you've ever called me. You gave it to me when we first started going out."

There was a long silence. Lisa exhaled with relief and was about to slam the phone down when the breathing whistled through the earpiece.

Another whisper.

"Lili."

The word cut Lisa like a dagger to the heart. *Lili.* That was the nickname Tommy had given her back when she was nineteen and madly in love. Lisa didn't know if there was any particular reason behind the nickname. It was just Tommy's little thing, the word he'd whispered in her ear first thing in the morning and last thing at night before they fell asleep. It hung around. She couldn't remember Tommy taking the name outside the house. Couldn't remember anyone else ever using it. In front of everyone else, she was always Lisa.

"It's a con," Lisa said. "This is a con, isn't it?"

The response was a muted croak, broken into clumsy, scattered syllables. "*Remember Menorca*?"

This time Lisa had to grab onto the bedside table to stop herself falling over.

"What did you say?"

"Remember Menorca?"

Menorca. Lisa and Tommy's first overseas holiday together. That was about twenty years ago now, long before marriage got its claws into their relationship. Menorca was a wild one and that was putting it mildly. Both Lisa and Tommy had partied like champion rock stars. Sex on the beach. Sex in the hot tub. Drink, drugs, debauchery. Very little sleep. They'd always remembered Menorca, particularly as their late twenties and early thirties saw them slowing down in life. Tommy the businessman. Lisa the serious-minded vet with the long, gruelling hours. They'd become exhausted. Exhausted with their lives, exhausted with each other. But whenever things got too dull, one of them would always lean in and intervene, whispering that two-word phrase, 'Remember Menorca?' That was their cue to do something spontaneous. Get shit-faced drunk. Have sex on the kitchen table (after clearing the plates off first). Choose the next holiday destination by pointing a finger on the map. Remember Menorca. It was Tommy and Lisa's thing and it could never belong to anyone else.

"You're dead," Lisa said. She let go of the table, recovered her sense of balance. "I buried you."

"Look outside."

"Why?"

"Go to the window. Look to your car."

That voice, she thought. It sounded like he was still in the river.

Lisa put the phone down on the table and walked over to the window. She pulled the curtains back. It wasn't much of a view. Her room faced onto the hotel's rear car park – a giant concrete square with white markings and little else to write home about. Lisa pushed her face onto the glass. Her eyes roamed the bland scenery, wandering fifty yards to the right where she'd parked her blue Corolla that afternoon.

"No."

Tommy Granger was standing in the narrow gap in between Lisa's car and a black Range Rover. He was there, just like he'd been there in between the trees in Victoria Park. The same man she'd loved for years, the same man she'd let drown. Tommy was back. His blond curls glowing in the dusk.

He waved at her.

Lisa retreated from the window. She was having a nightmare, that's all. A nightmare like all the other nightmares over the past twelve months. And when she woke up, she'd go back to Cathcart Cemetery, stand in front of the granite headstone and know for certain that Tommy Granger was dead and buried. Maybe she'd have to find someone shady to dig him up in the middle of the night. Take a picture of whatever was in that coffin just to be sure.

Lisa grabbed the phone off the table. Put the handset to her ear.

"What do you want?"

"Make it up to me."

"What? How?"

Silence.

"Hello?"

The disconnect tone rang in Lisa's ear.

She screamed in frustration and dropped the phone. It clattered hard off the bedside table. Lisa staggered towards the door, emerging yet again into the empty hotel corridor. She was running. She was slamming the button beside lift, trying to summon the damn thing from another floor. Then she was in the lift, going down from the second floor to reception.

Lisa's body flowed with adrenaline. Was this really happening?

The lift stopped. The doors slid open and she squeezed through the gap. Hurried past reception, not paying attention to anyone around her.

Lisa pushed through the door. She was outside now, walking around the hotel perimeter, making her way towards the rear car park. She was running again. Sprinting hard. A light rain began to fall.

"Tommy!"

Lisa reached the back car park and stopped dead. There was no sign of Tommy. The area was deserted except for an elderly couple talking to one other in a language that might have been German. They were loading two small suitcases into the back of their Ford Fiesta. They smiled at Lisa when they saw her and somehow she managed a feeble wave in return.

The rain grew heavier.

Lisa stood there, exposed to the elements, staring at the Corolla. Staring at the slim gap in between cars. Tommy Granger had been standing there minutes earlier. She'd seen him. She'd heard his voice.

There was no doubt now, Lisa thought.

Tommy was alive.

7

Lisa rang the doorbell and waited.

She was standing outside Iris's three-bedroom terraced house in Jordanhill. Lisa had returned to Glasgow after abandoning the vet congress in Edinburgh without attending a single lecture. The first thing she did after dropping her case off at the house was to call Malcolm at the clinic, telling him that she'd come down with a flu-like bug. That she needed a few days off work to shake off the worst of it. Malcolm told her to take all the time she needed. He spoke in a sympathetic tone. It was the one-year anniversary, Lisa thought. It was buying her a lot of pity.

What Lisa wanted, even more than time off, was to understand what had happened in the hotel room last night. Her first port of call was to visit Iris's house.

Footsteps approached from within the house. There was the brief rattle of a key being toggled in the lock, then the front door opened a few inches. Iris Granger's weathered face was blank as she peered through the narrow gap in the doorway. Her eyes lit up and she ventured outside onto the top step.

"Oh, it's you Lisa. Is everything alright darling?"

Iris was casually dressed in a pink t-shirt and black activewear leggings. The Nike trainers on her feet, along with a fine coating of sweat on her forehead, suggested she'd recently been on her beloved treadmill.

"Hi Iris," Lisa said. "Are you busy?"

Iris took a step back into the house, gesturing for Lisa to follow her. "Too busy for my daughter-in-law? I don't bloody well think so. What's wrong hen? Has something happened?"

"I just need a few minutes," Lisa said, following Iris into the house. "If that's okay?"

Iris nodded. "Aye, of course darling. Go into the living room – on you go. I just did my five kilometres upstairs and was rehydrating with a cuppa in front of the TV. You want something to drink? Tea? Coffee?"

"No thanks."

Lisa walked through the narrow hallway towards the living room. As she walked, she was aware of Iris right behind her. As close as Lisa's own shadow. Lisa glanced over her shoulder. Iris was smiling. Of course she was.

The tension broke when Lisa entered the living room and Shuggy the cat, a fourteen-year-old tabby and white, strolled across the couch to say hello to Lisa.

Lisa stroked Shuggy's back, running her hand down to the base of the tail. "Long time no see Shug."

The cat head-bumped Lisa's arm with impressive force. He was purring so loud it felt like the couch was vibrating.

"Take a seat darling," Iris said.

"Thanks."

As usual, Iris's home resembled a showhouse. For as long as Lisa had known her mother-in-law, the woman had kept the place immaculate even when she wasn't expecting company. Shuggy did his best to sabotage that and to make the place look a little more lived in, but Iris had strategically positioned scratching posts around the house and over time, the cat's will had been tamed. He'd learned to focus his destructive energies on the scratching posts instead of tearing the side of the couch to shreds or turning the carpet into confetti. The wood-panelled doors, the varnished flooring, the stained glass in the double glazing – the house was flawless. Only now, as she was well inside the house, did Lisa realise that she'd slipped off her shoes at the door without even thinking about it.

The living room radiator was on full blast. Lisa felt like her skin was slowly peeling off.

Another glance at the smiling Iris.

She shouldn't have come here.

"Want something to eat?" Iris asked. She picked up the remote control and turned off *Loose Women*. "A wee slice of carrot cake or a biscuit or something?"

"No thanks Iris. I can't stay long."

Iris's face creased up in confusion. She lowered herself onto the armchair, directly opposite the giant flatscreen TV. As she did, Shuggy hurried back across the living room, jumped onto her lap and curled up into a ball.

"What can I do for you sweetheart?"

Lisa took a seat on the couch. The sweat gathered on her brow and she was struggling to sit still due to the heat. "Something's been on my mind lately."

Iris's eyes flickered. It was as if a light had switched on somewhere at the back of her mind. "You can talk to me about anything Lisa. You're as much a daughter to me as Sheila and Kelly, I hope you know that. What's on your mind?"

"Tommy."

"I thought as much."

"It's not easy for me to come here like this," Lisa said, fidgeting with the straps of the bag sitting on her lap. "But I've been having bad dreams. Maybe it's the one-year anniversary thing, I don't know."

"Go on," Iris said, blinking slowly.

"It's like...I keep seeing him everywhere."

Iris sighed. She dabbed a finger at something in the corner of her eye. "I haven't told anyone this love but...

"What is it?"

"He comes to me in my dreams. Sometimes he's a wee boy again and we're back in the places we went on holiday with his dad and the girls. The caravan park, you know? Sometimes he's a man. But he's always smiling and looking right at me with those beautiful eyes. He had his dad's eyes, didn't he? But I feel like when he comes to me, he's trying to tell me something. I don't know what it is. Maybe he's just letting me know that he's alright."

Lisa flinched at a sudden crack from the floorboards upstairs.

"You okay darling?"

"Fine."

She glanced at the ceiling, wondering if she was truly alone in the house with Iris. This thought was immediately followed by a second creak from a loose floorboard. Was there someone up there?

Stop it, said the voice in Lisa's mind. Just stop it.

And yet she couldn't get the image of Tommy up there in his old bedroom. Not-dead Tommy, lying on the floor with his ear pressed to the ground. Listening to every word with a wicked grin on his two-timing face.

"That's not all," Lisa said, beads of sweat escaping down the side of her face. What must she look like to her mother-in-law? Did Iris seriously not know how hot it was inside the living room?

"What else?"

Lisa hesitated. "I keep imagining..."

"Uh-huh?"

"...imagining what he looked like."

Iris frowned. "Looked like? What do you mean?"

"On the slab. Dead. After they pulled him out of the river."

Iris shrunk back into the armchair, unable to conceal the sudden look of horror in her eyes. "Oh."

"You were the one who identified the body," Lisa said. "I couldn't do it but maybe if I had, if I knew what Tommy looked like, I'd stop seeing the pictures in my head. I'd stop filling in the blanks with all these awful details. Can you describe him to me?"

Can you?

Is he even dead? Or is he upstairs?

Lisa glanced at the ceiling. She couldn't keep doing that or it'd look suspicious.

Iris clutched the collar of her workout t-shirt. She pulled a face like she'd just tasted something sour. "Oh, for God's sake Lisa."

"I know. I know what it sounds like, I do."

Iris had insisted on identifying Tommy in the morgue that day. She didn't have to do it. The police told the family it wasn't necessary and that they could identify the body by fingerprints or dental records. They could use photos too. But a distraught Iris had insisted on going in there and taking one last look at her boy. She was the only one in the family who'd seen him. The two sisters said they wanted to remember Tommy as he was. Alive, vibrant and beautiful. Not as a decomposing corpse on a mortuary slab.

"He looked like he was sleeping."

Lisa raised an eyebrow. Sleeping? That sounded peaceful. Tempting, even. And yet Lisa could still hear Tommy hammering the glass with his hands and elbows. Using up the last of his strength. Peaceful? There was no way that Tommy could have looked peaceful in the morgue. Not after what happened.

She's lying, Lisa thought. The old bitch is lying.

"So pale," Iris continued. Her voice was down to a whisper and she stroked Shuggy's head while the little cat purred his approval. "But so peaceful. They dried his beautiful blond hair for me. So beautiful. That's all I can say Lisa. He looked like he was asleep."

Lisa sat there, nodding. "And there was never any doubt in your mind?"

"Doubt?"

"That it *was* Tommy."

Iris shook her head. "You don't think I'd recognise my own boy? Of course it was him. They pulled his car out the Clyde. Who else could it have been?"

"I saw him," Lisa said, locking eyes with Iris.

Iris sighed. She shifted in her seat a little, stretching over to a small bookcase behind the chair. She picked out a framed A4 print of Tommy sitting alongside a neat row of other family portraits. The picture in Iris's hand had been taken in a restaurant in Merchant City on Tommy's graduation day in 1999. Tommy was holding his grad certificate from Strathclyde University in one hand and a full pint of lager in the other. There was a crazed, relieved grin on his face.

"He's gone. It was just a dream Lisa."

Lisa shook her head. "I saw him."

"It's just your imagination," Iris said, putting the photo

back on the bookcase with a pained smile. "But I do understand why it's happening. He's everywhere, isn't he? He's sitting on the bus that drives past my window at least a dozen times a day. He's across the street. He's in the park when I go for a walk. If I walk past a barber's shop and there's a man with blond hair, it's always Tommy. At least for a second or two. When the anniversary is further behind us, I expect it'll stop."

"Iris," Lisa said in a quiet voice. "Tommy spoke to me."

Iris stood up and Shuggy jumped off her lap, trotting out of the living room with his tail in the air. "What's wrong with you Lisa? You still haven't told me exactly why you left the memorial early the other day?"

Lisa got to her feet too, threading the strap of her bag over her shoulder. Her back felt hot and damp. "You're hiding something from me."

Iris's jaw hit the floor. "What?"

"He found me in Edinburgh yesterday. Tommy found me. He called me in the room and spoke to me. At one point, he was standing outside the hotel beside my car."

"Oh you poor darling," Iris said, the hostility in her eyes melting into a look of profound pity. She reached for Lisa, then lowered her arms as if it was an intrusion of personal space. "It's just your mind. It's your mind playing tricks on you."

"He's alive," Lisa said. She was backing out of the living room. Iris tried to reach her again but Lisa flinched from her mother-in-law's grasping fingers. "Tommy's alive, isn't he? Did he tell you what happened?"

Iris clamped a hand over her mouth. Her eyes glistened with sorrow. "Lisa. I think you should leave."

Lisa retreated into the hallway, almost tripping over the cat while Iris followed at a distance. She felt a rush of panic.

Were they going to let her leave? Was someone about to run downstairs and grab her?

She had to get out of there.

"I'm going to pretend this never happened," Iris said. "Okay? But listen to me Lisa, please. You need to start taking better care of yourself sweetheart. Look at you – you're too skinny for God's sake. And don't think I can't smell the smoke and alcohol on your breath either. It's been hard for all of us, I know. But it's time to get back on track. Time to look forward, okay? I'm here if you need me."

Lisa slipped the shoes back on her feet. She grabbed the door handle, anticipating that it would be locked. But thank God it turned and she pulled the door open, rushing outside into the glorious fresh air.

She slammed the door shut behind her. Fumbled around in her pocket for the pack of cigarettes she'd picked up at the train station that morning. Lisa lit up, hands shaking. What on earth had she done? Had she really visited her broken-hearted mother-in-law and blurted out that her dead son was still alive?

It was crazy and yet, as she walked away from the house, feeling the rush of nicotine in her head, Lisa could feel someone staring at her from the upstairs bedroom window.

That was Tommy's old room.

8

Lisa didn't feel like going home right away so she took a bus into the city centre. The busy streets of Glasgow made her feel safe. Thousands of people filing past her, going about their business and making it look like any other ordinary day where dead spouses didn't come back.

She would have to go home sooner or later.

Make it later.

What Lisa really needed was a drink. After wandering the streets for a half-hour, she walked into Molly Malones, a traditional Irish pub on Hope Street. At the bar, Lisa ordered a glass of white wine and took it over to a corner table, one which allowed her a clear view of the door. Lisa sat on the bench, sipping the wine and listening to a tinny crackle of Irish trad music spill through the well-worn speakers on the walls. On a big screen next to the bar, the recent international rugby match between Scotland and Ireland was on replay.

Lisa put her iPhone in her bag, zipping it out of sight. She finished her wine and ordered another.

She spent the majority of the day in the pub. Drinking

wine and replaying the events of last night in the hotel room. The more she drank, the more she was willing to concede that it might have been nothing more than a vivid dream after all. That didn't stop her jumping out of her seat every time someone pushed the pub door open. Was she really expecting Tommy to be standing there in the doorway? Dripping wet. His waterlogged eyes roaming the pub in search of her.

She thought back to that hotel room in Edinburgh. The phone call. That *was* Tommy's voice, albeit a gargled and distorted version. The man in the car park. That was Tommy.

If it wasn't a dream, what else could it be?

It was simple. Either Tommy was a ghost (not that Lisa believed in ghosts) or what happened in Edinburgh was the beginning of an elaborate revenge plot concocted by the Granger clan. Not all of them (Granny Isobel and Ewan got a free pass). But Iris and her two daughters were different. Lisa hadn't seen her husband die after all. He was still alive when she swam away from the sinking Audi that morning. What if the people who'd appeared on the riverbank got Tommy out of there in time to resuscitate him? What if he managed to get out by himself? Did Tommy, stunned after his wife's betrayal, fake his death, fake his funeral and wait for the one-year anniversary to start chipping away at Lisa's sanity?

"You're insane," Lisa said, hearing the madness in her thoughts. She was drunk but she wasn't drunk enough to believe the bullshit swirling around her head. It was nonsense, plain and simple.

Most likely, it had been a dream.

She ordered another glass of wine. How many was that now? As she drank, she couldn't sit still. The fingernails of her left hand were tiny chisels chipping away at the legs of the wooden table.

What would a dead body look like after a year? Would she still recognise Tommy if she were to open his casket in Cathcart Cemetery? His blond curls – what was left of them? His cute little ears. The perfect nose. Lisa recalled a short quote she'd read in a true crime book. It was from a passage about decomposition – 'far from being dead, the rotting corpse is teeming with life.' How magnificent, she thought. Buried bodies, according to the book, were the cornerstone of a vast and complex ecosystem, interacting with the wider environment. Cadavers became insect colonies. Flies and maggots crawled all over the rotting flesh. Was that happening on Tommy's face right now? The man she'd loved for so long, reduced to an insect colony.

The wine glass was empty. Lisa forced herself back onto her feet and staggered over to the bar. The walk from table to bar was getting longer with each refill. The room and everything in it swirled. It had been a long time since Lisa had been this drunk in public. *Remember Menorca?* She leaned her elbows on the counter, grinning at the memories of that debauched trip to the Mediterranean island. The young guy working behind the bar gave Lisa a smile, indicating he'd be over in a second. He wasn't bad-looking. Bit young, perhaps. Lisa was trying to remember how to flirt when she caught an unexpected glimpse of her reflection in the mirror behind the bar.

God, she *was* thin. A skeleton with hair. All cheekbones and no face. A dead thing walking amongst the living.

"Yes gorgeous," the barman said, boogying over to Lisa with a big grin on his face. Looked like he was up for a bit of flirting. Maybe he was a skeleton fucker when he wasn't pulling pints of Guinness in an Irish pub. "What can I get you darling?"

But Lisa's hands were up, surrendering to the killjoy in her head. "Changed my mind. Thanks anyway."

Thanxsh anywaaay.

"No problem. You take it easy, okay?"

Lisa gave the barman a double thumbs up. Then she grabbed her bag off the table and staggered outside, leaning up against the wall to get some fresh air into her lungs. The world was spinning like a merry-go-round. Blurry human shapes rushed back and forth. The lights in the background were bright and dizzying. A car horn blared in the distance, followed by the sound of angry voices. Lisa took a deep breath, pulled the phone out her bag and unlocked the home screen There was a massive pile-up of missed calls from Deb and Risha, as well as others. There were some texts too. She'd get back to them all soon. Maybe tomorrow.

There was nothing from Iris. Lisa shrugged, even though she knew she was going to regret that visit in the morning.

Home, she thought. You need to go home.

Lisa managed to organise an Uber, which pulled into the side of the road a few minutes later. Despite worried looks from the driver in the rearview, Lisa managed to get through the short journey without throwing up in the backseat. Thank God, he didn't try and make conversation either.

She locked the front door and checked it several times over. Then she was in the kitchen, shoving bread into the toaster, piling a small mountain of toast and raspberry jam onto a plate. She took the plate upstairs and watched an episode of *The Big Bang Theory* on Netflix while she rammed the toast into her mouth.

It wasn't long before Lisa's eyelids grew heavy. She just

about had the presence of mind to turn off the TV and bedside light before burrowing under the covers.

She heard the plate fall off the bed. Great, she thought. A few burned crusts to add to the mess on the floor.

Despite her exhaustion, Lisa couldn't fall asleep once the lights were off. She lay on her back, looking up at the cracks in the ceiling. Everything was still spinning. Thank God, she wasn't due in work tomorrow.

Her stomach lurched.

Lisa tossed back the sheets, ran into the ensuite bathroom and threw up all the toast and wine. It was brutal. She felt like she was turning herself inside out.

Afterwards, she lay on the cold floor. It was nice down there. She ran her fingers over the blue and white diamond pattern on the tiled surface, remembering how Tommy's blond hairs used to always show up on the floor, in the sink and in the bath. God, she missed him. Or at least missed how they used to be. The hairs were a source of constant irritation and Lisa was always fishing them out, telling Tommy to check for himself once in a while. She'd even accused him of dropping hairs in the sink to annoy her.

Her fingers ran over the smooth surface of the tiles but came up empty. There was nothing of Tommy left in the bathroom. Lisa recalled a mad bout of cleaning up and vacuuming in the days immediately after the crash. The house had been spotless, at least for a week or two.

With a groan, Lisa climbed back to her feet and rinsed her mouth out with cold water. She walked back to the bedroom and fell face first onto the mattress. All she wanted to do was sleep for days. To hide under the covers. Then, once she got her head straight, she'd be able to go back to work at the clinic and put in the long hours. She'd also start prepping for the move out of Glasgow.

Lisa rolled onto her back, her mind racing like a bullet train. She was still thinking about human decomposition and the maggots in Tommy's eye sockets. That picture was still in her mind's eye when she finally succumbed to the exhaustion.

Lisa sat bolt upright in bed, glancing at the digital clock on the table.

2.29AM.

The landline was ringing and it sounded like a freight train running through Lisa's skull. She grabbed the handset before the noise split her head in two.

"Hello?"

No answer. Lisa, still groggy, was about to slam the phone down when she heard a noise like an insect running around inside the handset. Something else followed – coughing. Gasping. Someone frantic for air.

Lisa screamed. She slammed the phone down and searched for the lamp switch beside the bed. Her clawing fingers took forever to find the switch.

She sat there, covered in sweat. Staring at the phone and unsure of what to do next. Call the police? The Ghost-busters? Maybe she could call Deb or Risha but it was so late. They'd be in bed and it wasn't fair to call them after she'd ignored them for so long.

Damn it.

Lisa flinched at another noise. This time it came from outside the house. From the street. From the front door?

Her body shook uncontrollably. She threw the covers off her legs and raced around the upstairs of the house, hitting switches and turning on all the lights. Everything looked better with the lights on.

What next?

Go to the kitchen. Get a big knife.

Lisa heard a sound like footsteps on the garden path. She was certain of it now. There was someone outside the house.

She stood frozen at the top of the staircase, staring wide-eyed at the front door.

"I know you're there," Lisa said, placing her foot on the top step. The staircase creaked and it sounded like the roof was about to collapse on her head. Lisa descended the stairs slowly, touching down in the hallway and hitting the light switch. The warm glow that enveloped her felt no more comforting than the dark.

She couldn't stop shaking.

From the hall, Lisa crept into the living room. She stopped at the window, took a deep breath and pulled back the curtains. The street was quiet and deserted, as it should be at this hour. There was no one outside the house or standing at the front door. No flatbed trucks carrying an angry mob of Granger associates armed with torches and pitchforks.

Lisa closed the curtains. Had she dreamt the phone call too? Were the nightmares becoming so bad that she was mistaking them for reality? She walked to the front door, turned the key and the metallic clicking noise sent a chill down her spine. There was nothing between her and what was outside.

What if he's hiding?

The garden was empty when Lisa opened the door. There was no menacing figure standing on the doorstep or on the path or waiting down by the gate. Nothing but a mild breeze that whistled past Lisa's ears.

She was about to close the door when she noticed the envelope. It was sitting on the top step.

Lisa squatted down, picked it up. She tiptoed back into the house and angled the envelope directly under the hall light so she could read the text. There was a strange design on the front. An untidy collage of bold and small letters that appeared to have been cut from various newspaper and magazine headlines. These letters were glued to the envelope to form a clumsy, childish-looking header.

MaKe It Up tO Me

Lisa felt dizzy. She closed the door, took the envelope to the bottom of the staircase and sat down.

She pierced the envelope and pulled out a sheet of unfolded A4 paper. It was a typed note.

"Christ," she whispered. Then she began to read:

Make it up to me.

Random Acts of Kindness, part 1 – WRITE A LETTER

Lili,

You must make amends for what you did. You have no idea how important it is to fix your wrongdoing. To atone. Start by writing an anonymous letter to my mother. Tell her you went into the water that day and swam up to the car. Tell her you chose not to save her darling boy and instead watched me drown. Tell her how scared I was. Spare no details. Let her know what my face looked like. Tell her about the sounds I made as I drowned.

Honesty is kindness. Even when it hurts.

Post the letter first thing in the morning. I'll be watching closely.

Do this and you might not go to jail.

Tommy

9

Lisa glanced at the clock.

4.21AM.

Three minutes since she'd last checked.

The MacBook Pro was sitting on her naked legs – legs that had noticeably thinned out over the past year. It had been sitting there for an hour, lid open, a blank Word document with a single bold heading at the top:

LETTER FOR IRIS:

That was the extent of Lisa's masterpiece so far. It had taken her all that time to get those three words down on the page. It had taken her just as long to decide whether to write the letter in the first place.

She was sitting on the couch in the living room, her feet propped up on the Moroccan pouf that she'd brought back from her final holiday with Tommy in the South of France. That was two years ago. All the lights in the house were on. According to the instructions, Lisa had to write the letter to Iris and post it first thing in the morning.

The 'Make It Up To Me' instructions were beside her on the couch.

Lisa's fingers slid off the keyboard. She closed her eyes, inhaling the cocktail of foul odours running loose around the house. It wasn't just Lisa's physical appearance that had gone down the pan lately. There was a skyscraper-high stack of dirty dishes in the kitchen sink. The dishwasher had broken down months ago and she'd never bothered getting someone in to fix it. Lisa had gotten into the habit of eating off plastic plates even though she knew it was a disaster for the environment. She didn't have the energy to improve her habits even though she knew it was no excuse. There were discarded piles of clothes everywhere. Takeaway boxes. Chocolate wrappers. Thick layers of dust lining the surfaces in every room. The job of sorting out the mess was getting bigger and bigger but for Lisa, it was always 'I'll do it later'.

She turned her attention back to the screen. Back to the cursor blinking impatiently.

Once she'd typed out the letter, *if* she ever got around to typing it, she'd print it out on the Canon upstairs, assuming the printer hadn't run out of ink. Lisa would then handle the print copy with gloves. She'd seen enough TV shows and films and true crime documentaries to know that her fingerprints had to stay off the paper and the envelope. The gloves were sitting on the coffee table in front of her. Ready to go. There was a cloth for wiping down the envelope.

Her hands went back to the keyboard.

She began to type.

Dear Iris,

Lisa stopped at the sound of a car door slamming shut on the street. She heard the muted growl of an engine firing into life from a few houses down. Somebody going to work already? There was birdsong too, breaking out in spurts in the back garden.

"Make it up to me," Lisa said, reading the front of the

envelope beside her. "How about you go fuck yourself instead?"

She reached for the glass of water on the table. Took a sip. The ibuprofen she'd taken earlier was working, holding back the inevitable hangover that would show up belated in the morning. A couple more of those ibuprofen pills wouldn't go amiss but Lisa couldn't be bothered getting up to go to the medicine drawer. What she needed were proper sleeping pills to knock her out at night. Another thing to add to the to-do list.

4.32AM.

Loosening her joints, Lisa cracked her knuckles. Then she stretched her fingers out as far as they could go.

"This time."

She typed the first sentence and after a shaky start, the words poured out of her. It was painful at first, then liberating to write a confession. She sat forward on the couch. Alert. Fully awake, like she'd just swallowed a pot of black coffee. She tore through page after page in a frenzy, unloading everything to the point where her fingers couldn't keep up with her brain. It's an anonymous note, she told herself. Only half a confession. She could write whatever she wanted and so she did.

The short confession ended up being five pages long.

10

Lisa woke up on the couch, drowning in a nest of blankets.

She kicked the blankets onto the floor and when she lifted her head off the cushion, she saw an empty bag of salt and vinegar crisps at her feet. Last night's dinner. Crumbs peppered all over the couch. A half-full glass of wine and an open bottle sitting on the table beside her.

The landline was ringing. When would she learn to take the phone off the hook at night? To turn her mobile off too, or at least put it on silent mode?

Lisa manoeuvred herself into a sitting position and her joints cracked in protest at this sudden interruption. Sunlight intruded through chinks in the curtains. A quick glance at the clock told Lisa that it was just after midday. At best, she'd had about four hours uninterrupted sleep. That was pretty good going.

The phone continued to scream behind Lisa's head. She grabbed the handset and spoke in a tired, raspy voice.

"Hello?"

"Lisa? Is that you sweetheart? Is everything okay?"

Iris's voice sounded urgent. Here we go, Lisa thought,

feeling a sudden urge to throw up. She'd been expecting this call ever since posting the anonymous confession yesterday morning. Fortunately for Lisa, it *was* just a phone call and not a knock on the door. Be grateful for small mercies.

"Hi Iris. I'm fine."

"I've been trying to reach you on your mobile all morning," Iris said, her voice getting harder. "Calls, texts, voicemails. You're a nightmare to get a hold of these days Lisa darling, you really are. You want to try picking up your phone once in a while, eh?"

Lisa didn't know where she'd left her iPhone. It was somewhere – in her bag, in a pocket, plugged into one of a dozen or so charging points lying around the house. Screw it – it always turned up in the end.

"Is something wrong?"

"Are you sitting down?" Iris asked. "Trust me sweetheart. You're better off sitting down before you hear this."

Lisa felt like she was glued to the couch with stale sweat. "I'm sitting. What happened?"

"I got a letter this morning."

"Uh-huh."

Lisa didn't have the will or energy to conjure up a tone of shock or surprise.

"It's some kind of confession," Iris said. "Written by someone who claims to have, oh God, by someone who claims they dove into the river after Tommy's crash. Aww Lisa, it's horrible. It goes into all sorts of gruesome, twisted detail. I'll spare you that much."

"Tell me."

There was a long pause on the other end.

"Tell me," Lisa repeated. "What does it say?"

"Are you sure you want to hear this?"

Iris's voice was hoarse and thick. Lisa guessed her

mother-in-law had been crying all morning. Either that or she was coming down with something.

"I'm sure," Lisa said.

"Acchh, it's sick. They're saying they swam right up to the passenger side where Tommy was. Said they watched Tommy hitting the windows with his fists, begging for help."

There was a pause. Sounded like Iris was trying to catch her breath. Lisa thought it sounded a bit like what she'd been hearing on those strange calls she'd been receiving lately.

"They watched him drown," Iris said, her voice trembling. "And they did nothing to help him. Nothing Lisa, they did nothing. They could have saved my son and they...oh God, his eyes, they said, his eyes were..."

"Go on," Lisa said, ignoring the muffled sob in her ear. "What else does it say?"

"His eyes were like two swollen balloons. His skin was rubbery. Jesus Christ, they've written a bloody essay on it, adding in all the minute details. It all comes down to the same thing in the end. They left my boy to die down there. And now they've sent this letter to taunt me. What for? Do they want me to go mad? To have nightmares for the rest of my life?"

They called it a random act of kindness, she thought, thinking back to what it said on the letter. Honesty is kindness.

Like hell it is.

She reached for the wine bottle and took a swig. It tasted foul. Like it had been sitting open like that for weeks.

"Are you there?" Iris asked.

"I'm here," Lisa answered, wincing as she put the bottle on the floor. "Don't worry about this, Iris. I got a letter too."

Iris's voice shot up several octaves to a surprised squeak. "You got a letter too?"

"Yep."

"When?"

"This morning."

"You're joking," Iris said. "What does it say?"

"Same thing as yours."

"Why didn't you tell me sooner? For God's sake darling. Why on earth did you make me read mine out loud?"

"I had to be sure we had the same letter."

"Bloody hell."

Lisa stretched both legs out, the joints popping as she placed them on the armrest. "Don't lose any sleep over it, Iris. I won't."

"What? How can you say that? This is serious."

"It's a prank," Lisa said, inserting a jolt of assertiveness into her voice. She knew she had to shut this thing down. Shut Iris down before she started getting other people involved. Sheila and Kelly probably knew but with any luck, Lisa could stop Iris from contacting the police if she hadn't already. "It's trolls."

"Trolls?"

"Deb told me about it. Apparently, it's pretty common amongst sickos. They scour the obituary sections looking for something interesting to cling onto."

Iris made a tut-tutting noise. "I've never heard of it."

"Ghoulish as hell," Lisa said. "These trolls, they take note of the deceased, find out how they died and it all spirals from there. They look up the family, dig up whatever info they can and then mark their calendars. The anniversaries start rolling around and that's usually when they start their little reign of terror and torment. Some do it for money. Others? Power. Kicks. That's how they get their rocks off."

Iris gasped. "Are you serious? There's people out there who do *that*?"

Lisa's head fell back onto the couch. She closed her eyes and saw Tommy hammering his fists off the car window. His eyes, grotesque. Bug-like with panic. "It's a sick world we live in."

"Aww, that can't be true. Surely that can't be true."

Okay. You'd rather have the truth Iris? Tommy told me to write the letter. Saint Tommy the angel has come back from the dead to purify my soul and cleanse me of all sin. Do you believe me now? And no, I didn't receive a letter – I'm just trying to cover my tracks here. Should have printed an extra copy, just in case anyone wanted to check. That seems obvious now, but I'm new to all this.

Of course, Lisa thought, that wasn't the only option. There was still the possibility that Tommy had gotten out of the river alive. That he was holed up in Iris's house, playing the long revenge game. Maybe he was even standing beside the Granger matriarch as she put on a tortured old woman act for Lisa on the phone. Both of them, their faces scrunched up, trying not to laugh at the dumb bitch who'd left Tommy for dead. If that was true, if Iris and the Grangers were trying to break Lisa, then the old woman knew fine well that Lisa didn't receive a letter. But what else could Lisa do? She had to take that risk and play along. She didn't think that Iris and the Grangers, if they were orchestrating some kind of revenge mission against her, were ready to give away their advantage.

"I'm calling the police if it happens again," Iris said.

Lisa breathed a sigh of relief. At least the old woman hadn't reported it. "I threw my letter in the bin. Don't give them any attention and it'll go away. It's like they say on the Internet – don't feed the trolls."

Iris made a brief whimpering noise. "I don't understand some people. How sick do you have to be to do something like that? Torturing people who've lost someone dear to them."

Lisa's eyes narrowed. "I have to go Iris. Got an appointment to keep."

"Right you are darling. Let me know if anything else happens, okay? If you get a letter or a phone call, I want to be the first to know about it."

"Will do. Bye."

Lisa hung up. She stood up and walked stiffly to the kitchen, grabbing the last bottle of unopened wine off the worktop. She looked around. The kitchen was a ghost town. All the cupboards were bare and that meant she'd have to go to the shops soon. Stock up on supplies.

With the bottle tucked under her arm, Lisa went back to the couch and pulled all the blankets over her legs again.

She turned on the TV. Within ten minutes, she was fast asleep.

11

Lisa continued to experience broken bouts of sleep that left her feeling exhausted in the mornings. She had no trouble nodding off on the couch but it was impossible for her to get any kind of significant rest. Going to bed was a waste of time, one that always saw her back on the couch with the blankets and a bottle, watching TV and catching ten minutes here and there. Maybe a few hours on a good night.

Exhausted, she finally scheduled an appointment with her local GP. Sleeping pills. That's what she needed for a proper night's rest and to get her energy back.

The appointment with Dr Claire Thompson was booked for Wednesday morning. Lisa cleaned up as best she could. She took a shower, her first in a week, and she slapped a little makeup over her skeletal features. Still, she couldn't hide the shadows under her eyes. The drooping shoulders wouldn't correct themselves either.

She drove down to the clinic and explained to Dr Thompson that she was having trouble staying asleep. Lisa made a point of talking in the calm, rational voice she used at work when talking to clients. She lied about the reasons for needing the pills. Told the doctor it was work related stress.

Dr Thompson was happy to prescribe Zolpidem for the short term. She also encouraged Lisa to take more time off work and to make good use of that time by exercising and avoiding caffeine and other stimulants. Lisa nodded, made it clear she understood. As the appointment came to an end, Dr Thompson once again stressed the importance of avoiding stimulants. She also said she'd like to see Lisa gain a little weight. Lisa told her she was working on it and a follow up appointment was booked in a fortnight.

Lisa thanked the doctor and went on her way.

Whilst in the chemist waiting for her prescription, Lisa sent an email to Malcolm at work. It was short and sweet. She let him know that the doctor had advised an extended period off work. Already, it felt like ages since Lisa had been at the clinic and she felt guilty for not being there to lend her support. Malcolm's reply was swift. *Take all the time you need.* Lisa replied, thanking him and underneath she sent out a separate request for a meeting next week. Out of hours. Coffee and a quick chat – her treat. She didn't mention that she wanted to talk to him about her leaving the practice. Malcolm was a good guy. He deserved to hear the news in person.

After collecting the prescription, Lisa decided to go home and research some vet practices in the north of England. On the way, she popped into a Tesco to stock up on supplies. She loaded up on bread, pasta and snacks. And even though she wasn't supposed to drink with the sleeping pills, she bought a few bottles of white wine.

Just in case.

Standing at the self-checkout, Lisa felt a sudden pinprick of heat touch the back of her neck. The sensation began to rake down her skin like a sharp fingernail. Was somebody watching her? The desire to turn around and check was overwhelming. But she held on without looking, telling herself that it was the exhaustion. The paranoia was thriving and would continue until she had the energy to fight it off.

She scanned her items, throwing everything into the reusable bag she'd taken out of the boot of the car. As she packed, Lisa glanced back and forth around the shop. No one was looking at her. There was no wet man with blond curls.

Of course not, she thought. The wet man is in Cathcart Cemetery and his eyes are full of maggots.

Lisa hurried away, the wine bottles clinking off each other in the bag. She walked through the sliding doors and it felt good to be outside again. A light drizzle of rain had begun to fall. The aisles inside Tesco were too narrow, Lisa decided. The other people, too close for comfort. In the future she'd shop at a quieter time of day.

As she walked to the car, Lisa noticed a sports supplies shop directly across the street from the supermarket. After dropping off the bags in the boot, she crossed the street on a sudden whim. Lisa opened the door and there was a loud chime to announce her arrival. The smell of rubber from bike tyres and brand-new trainers was potent. It was a small shop, packed mostly with football and rugby equipment. Lisa walked around for a few minutes. She found herself drawn to a corner display of aluminium baseball bats at the back wall. As she stood in front of the display, she glanced through the shop window towards the Tesco. She recalled the feeling of being watched.

Without giving it much thought, Lisa pulled two bats from the display. She took them over to the counter, telling the chatty young female assistant that they were for her kids. A belated birthday present for the elder.

It was a silly buy but Lisa felt better for having the bats in her possession. She'd keep one in the house, the other in the car.

Again, just in case.

There were no more stops. Lisa returned home fifteen minutes later and locked the front door behind her. She closed the curtains in the living room and the house fell into a private, premature dusk. After unpacking the shopping, she checked her phone and noticed that Malcolm had replied to her last message. He'd taken her off the rota for next week and left things open so she could have more time off if required. Also, he'd be delighted to catch up and have coffee next week. Lisa smiled. Malcolm was a bit too flirty with the nurses and sometimes with Lisa, but his heart was in the right place. She hoped he'd be okay about her leaving the business. A business that they'd built together from scratch and had even talked about expanding. He could still do all that, but he'd have to do it without Lisa.

There were no more scenarios in which she could envision herself staying in Glasgow. Leaving wasn't an option. It was an inevitability.

Lisa noticed a text from Ewan in the pile of unopened messages. He'd written in all caps and without punctuation. The poor kid, Lisa thought. What chance did he have with Sheila as the only parent? Ewan wanted to let Lisa know that it was good to see her at Tommy's memorial and he hoped she was okay after going home early. Lisa typed out a reply, thanking Ewan for his concern. She suggested they meet up soon for lunch in the city centre but didn't commit to a date. Lisa would also have to tell Ewan that she was leaving Glasgow. That wouldn't be easy. Tommy had loved the boy like a son and Lisa felt a connection there too. More so since Tommy's death.

Malcolm, Ewan, Risha, Deb, and more – there were a lot of people she was going to have to disappoint.

She signed off with a small kiss to Ewan. Told him she'd get back to him about that lunch date.

With all the shopping unpacked, Lisa took a bottle of Gris into the dimly lit living room. It was like walking into the aftermath of a bombsite. Lisa tossed one of the baseball bats on the floor to add to the mess. There, she thought. Something to hit Tommy over the head with the next time he wants to play midnight postman. But the damn mess. She'd get around to cleaning up, maybe as early as tomorrow. She just needed to sit down and it was okay to drink a little wine because she wasn't going to take any sleeping pills until at least a half hour before going to bed.

Lisa flopped onto the couch and poured herself a small glass. The urge to go back to Cathcart Cemetery arose in her all of a sudden. Why did that keep happening? What did she expect to find this time around? Tommy's grave all dug up? The headstone tipped over, a mound of earth piled sky-high and a coffin with the lid propped open? Maybe even a note taped to the lid:

Popped out to mindfuck the wife. Back soon. Tommy X

She sat in the gloomy living room, closed off to the outside world. Starting the work she was supposed to do was harder than she thought. Lisa opened the lid of the laptop but couldn't find the will to get anything going. Every hour or two, she'd get up to check the front and back doors were locked. Back in the living room, a call came through on her mobile. It was Risha. Knowing that she'd batted her friend away long enough, Lisa relented and picked it up.

"Hi Risha."

Risha sounded like a mother scolding her child for staying outside too long. "Lisa. What the hell's going on with you? Why won't you reply to my texts?"

"Sorry about that sweetie," Lisa said in a calm voice. "I'm fine. It's exhaustion really, I think. I went to the doctor's today for some sleeping pills."

Lisa heard Risha sigh. A slow hiss of disappointment. "For God's sake," Risha said, apparently ignoring the news about the GP visit. "We're supposed to be friends, aren't we? Deb and I were about to stage an intervention and break your front door down."

Lisa shivered at the thought. "I just need a good night's sleep. After that, everything will start getting better."

"Are you off work right now?"

"I've got a week as things stand. But I'm good to take more time if I need it."

"You sound wrecked Lisa."

"Sounds about right."

"And what else is going on?" Risha asked. The words came flying out like bullets from a machine gun. "Don't say nothing either. That memorial was killing you the other day, don't think I didn't notice. You looked like you were going to pass out if you stayed another minute. How much do you weigh at the moment? Are you monitoring your weight?"

Lisa closed her eyes and tried to concentrate. "I'll be fine. I just need to sleep."

"And put on some weight."

"Yes. And put on some weight."

A pause.

"Want me to come over tonight?" Risha asked. Although Lisa wasn't sure it was a question. "I can cook for us. We can invite Deb, have a laugh and watch some terrible films or something. Like we used to do, remember?"

Lisa remembered but it felt like years ago. Bad Movie Night. A girls' night in where the only requirement was to bring along some of the worst movies ever committed to the DVD bargain bin. Movies so bad they were brilliant. But that was a long time ago. That's how it felt to Lisa.

"I'm going to have an early night," she said. "But we'll do that soon."

Risha spoke in a pleading voice. "You don't have to do any work. I'll cook. I'll clean up. I'll let Deb know we're doing it. C'mon Lisa, it'll be fun."

"I'm sure it will be. Maybe next weekend, okay?"

"Definitely next weekend."

"Thanks for calling – it's great to hear your voice."

"Answer my calls Lisa, okay? Reply to my texts. That's all I ask."

"Will do."

After hanging up, Lisa stared at the MacBook on the cluttered coffee table. Maybe after a nap she'd find the energy to get some work done. New job. New place to live. New beginning. It was supposed to be exciting and energising but at that moment, it was just another thing to do. But it *was* exciting and Lisa would get on board soon. Maybe tomorrow. She was already fantasising about moving day. About hiring a company to take care of all the legwork. The house, gradually being stripped of all connection to Tommy.

Lisa stretched out on the couch, pulled the blankets over her head and fell into a restless sleep.

It was dark when she woke up. Lisa sat up, wondering if she needed those sleeping pills after all. She glanced around the living room, noticing the glint of the shiny new baseball bat at the foot of the couch. She recalled the embarrassment of buying it and the one in the boot.

Soon enough, she'd move out. Give the bats to a charity shop.

Lisa pushed herself off the couch, went over to the window and peeled back the curtains. It wasn't quite dark yet. The long summer days were a source of comfort, still bright at around ten o'clock at night. She glanced across the street. Saw a wall of closed curtains on the other houses, a whisper of electric light seeping through the window frame.

Lisa's eyes wandered back to the gate. Up the garden path towards the house. And then she saw it, sitting there on the top step.

Another envelope.

She froze, just for a second. Then she felt an explosion of urgency and ran across the room, grabbed the baseball bat and charged towards the front door. Lisa flung it open, the bat cocked over her shoulder in firing position.

"Where are you?"

She was alone.

Lisa hurried down the steps, landing on the garden path. She looked both ways, the bat still ready to go in her hands. The street was quiet. Darkness was rolling into the neighbourhood, suffocating the daylight. Lisa turned back to the house, picked up the A4 envelope and looked at it. The title had once again been created with a mishmash of old print letters.

mAKe iT Up to Me

Lisa brought the envelope into the house, closing the door and locking it. She checked the lock, counting out five checks before she was satisfied.

She sat down on the couch, staring at the envelope in her hand. Then her finger sliced the top open. Another typed note waited inside. Lisa pulled it out and began to read.

Make it up to me

Random acts of kindness, Part 2 - MONEY

Take a thousand pounds out of your bank account and donate it to charity. Do it online. Do it now. Then fill a big bag with twenty-pound notes and walk around the city centre, giving the twenties to homeless people. Take all day to do it. Give your money away with a smile.

I'll be watching.

Tommy

Lisa put the letter down on the table. She read it a second time from afar. A third time. Then she picked up her laptop and browsed the local charity websites that came up with a quick Google search. After about ten minutes browsing, she donated a thousand pounds to a Scottish children's charity. It was an anonymous donation.

That was easy enough, she thought. Expensive, but easy.

Lisa was determined not to crack. To react badly to the note, to the demands, to the overall situation that she knew for sure wasn't a dream. Didn't she deserve to suffer for what she'd done? There was no chance of sleep now. He was still out there, she thought, watching the house. Lisa sat up all night with the TV blaring at twice the required volume. She took the phone off the hook and turned off her mobile.

The next day, a sluggish Lisa took the bus into the city centre. At an ATM, she drew out three hundred pounds in twenties and walked up and down Sauchiehall Street, then Buchanan Street and Argyle Street, handing out money to those in need. Every now and then, she'd feel that pinprick of heat flaring up on the back of her neck. It was as if someone was holding a magnifying glass to the sun and concentrating the hot rays on Lisa.

She'd stop. Turn around. No one was paying her any attention.

Later that day, Lisa made an appointment to give blood. She was registered in the system but she hadn't donated in a while so she booked a date for next week. That was something else, wasn't it? Something good.

After a long day on her feet, Lisa walked into Buchanan Galleries shopping centre. She took the lift to the top floor and sat in a café with a strong black coffee and a complimentary sugary biscuit. She took her laptop out of her bag, connected it to the Wi-Fi and browsed, seeking out other philanthropical tasks that needed doing. After making a shortlist, Lisa applied for a role as a 'caring caller' in the local community. It was only an hour a week, visiting an elderly person, sitting with them and keeping them company. But it *was* a good thing. These were the kinds of people who were lonely, unwell, isolated and without friends or spouse.

Lisa filled in the application and sent it off. She took a sip of coffee, her eyes scanning the sea of faces in the food court.

How am I doing Tommy?

12

The next morning, Lisa found another letter at the door. It came less than twenty-four hours after she'd donated a thousand pounds to charity, personally handed out hundreds of pounds to the homeless, and signed up to be a caring caller.

She was sitting at the bottom of the stairs with the third letter still unopened in her hands. Her lips felt numb. Lisa couldn't recall if she'd taken a sleeping pill last night. That was silly, she knew it was. Downright stupid in fact, since she'd consumed two glasses of wine in the evening. At least two. There'd been coffee at some point too. Not to be taken with stimulants, remember? Why couldn't she remember this stuff when it mattered? Why couldn't she take care of herself like a normal human being?

Lisa opened the letter. Read the typed message several times over.

Make it up to me

Random Acts of Kindness, Part 3 – DONATE CLOTHING

It's clean out time. Give all your clothes to charity. Do it now, all of them. All your jewellery too. Do it today and start all over again. You have much to clear out.

Still watching you,

Tommy.

The letter slipped through her fingers.

"Okay."

She walked to the front door, desperate for a lungful of fresh air. But standing on the top step wasn't enough. Before Lisa knew it, she was out on the pavement, walking in her bare feet with only a pink t-shirt and her underwear on.

She looked up. The sun was hidden behind the clouds, dimming the bright colours and making the sky glow a distant shade of grey.

Lisa saw him at the end of the street. The man. This was the man who'd dropped off the note. He had the same curly blond hair as Tommy and he was facing Lisa.

"I'm coming," she said. "Wait for me."

Lisa's listless walk exploded into a frantic sprint. As she ran, she envisioned herself as a racing supercar going from nought to sixty in two seconds. This was more like the old Lisa. A force of nature. The person she'd once been, even before Tommy.

Lisa stumbled off the kerb, bouncing onto the road. The surface was hostile. A myriad of sharp objects snapped at the soles of her feet. Lisa paid little attention to the pain. She tripped seconds later, recovered her balance but when she looked up again, Tommy was gone. There was only the long stretch of empty, suburban road ahead. There was nothing where he'd been standing.

The half-naked Lisa came to a sudden halt.

"Oh shit."

She glanced left and right but there were no horrified faces gathered at the neighbouring windows. Gawping at her with pity in their eyes. Lisa wasn't about to wait for them. She turned and ran back to her house, the heels of her feet digging into the jagged grooves on the pavement. Lisa didn't care about the scrapes or cuts she'd acquired. She just wanted to get out of sight and fast.

She ran up the path, slammed the front door behind her.

Lisa stood in the hall, staring into a house that didn't feel safe. She walked over to the stairs, felt the sting of the wounds on her feet. She picked up today's note and read it again. Part three, donate clothing. That was *very* Tommy. He'd always thought of Lisa as a bit of a hoarder when it came to clothes and other things. Even had the nerve to say she was materialistic, obsessed with *things*, mostly clothes and jewellery. He'd been teasing her. Sort of.

"Okay. I'll do it."

Lisa was about to go upstairs when she heard her iPhone ringing from the kitchen. She walked over to the charger on the worktop and glanced at the screen. Deb's tanned, grinning face stared back at her. Shit, Lisa thought. Deb was on a mission. Lisa was supposed to have called her back yesterday or the day before, but after reading this latest note, she couldn't handle a conversation.

"Sorry Deb."

Maybe tomorrow.

She walked back into the hallway. Lisa knew she was going to run out of friends if she didn't stop acting like such an arsehole. Pushing them away. Punishing them for caring about her. But she was too tired. Too busy. Lisa's first caring caller visit was scheduled, fast-tracked for later that afternoon. The background checks had cleared quickly and the company had been in touch, giving Lisa the all clear and letting her know that she'd be meeting eighty-three-year-old

Annette Calderwood at her home in nearby Anniesland. One of the organisers, an enthusiastic Englishman called Brian, had offered to accompany Lisa on her first visit to Annette's house. Lisa turned the offer down, insisting that she was okay to go on her own.

But before anything else, Lisa had to go upstairs and empty her wardrobe. That's what Tommy wanted. That's what he'd get.

She grabbed a roll of binbags on her way upstairs. Then she went to work, pulling clothes out of the main wardrobe and three sets of drawers, throwing them onto the bed. Dresses, coats, t-shirts, underwear, shoes – everything had to go. Most of the clothes had unique stories behind them but Lisa put up a mental dam, blocking the memories. Memories would slow her down. Make it harder. They were just garments after all. She was moving away and so it was a good time to shed her skin. New clothes, new country, new job, new Lisa. The person who'd let Tommy drown would be no more.

This was a good thing.

She left only a few basic items hanging in the wardrobe. One pair of Levi's jeans, a couple of her favourite Nike t-shirts, a jumper, her trainers and a pair of smart shoes. Tommy wouldn't mind her keeping that much. After all, she needed *something* to wear.

Lisa filled a dozen large bags with clothes and dropped them off at the front door. The great clear out was done and whoopty fucking doo, she thought. She felt as light as a feather, one that was encased in lead. Her wardrobe and drawers, once a source of joy, were stripped almost bare.

How am I doing Tommy?

Lisa took a hot shower after all the work was done. She dried off, rolled some anti-perspirant under her arm, put on one of her few remaining t-shirts, along with the jeans and trainers. Finally, she tied her hair back into a bun.

She stood in front of the full-length mirror. These days it was like there was a ghost looking back at her. The healthy colour of Lisa's old face was gone, replaced by a ghoulish white veneer. She put on a little lipstick. Some blusher to restore the glow in her cheeks. She didn't want the old woman in Anniesland to think that a vampire had come to visit her.

All she really wanted to do was go back to the couch. To burrow under the blankets and wait the day out.

Lisa walked downstairs, gathered up the binbags and tossed them into the boot of her Toyota Corolla . She saw the baseball bat stashed in there. Felt another twinge of embarrassment. She paused beside the driver's door, looking towards the end of the street where she'd seen Tommy earlier in the day.

"Crazy," she mumbled. "You're going crazy."

Lisa drove ten minutes to the nearest Salvation Army shop. She walked inside, offering her bags to the elderly lady working behind the counter.

"Just some clothes," she said. "And a bit of jewellery."

The old woman smiled, grateful for the contribution. As she voiced her thanks, Lisa felt the back of her neck flaring up again. She glanced around the shop while the woman continued to talk and praise Lisa for her generosity. There were only a few people inside the Salvation Army store. A twenty-something woman browsing the decorative plates and cutlery stacks. A sandy-haired boy of about six was glued to her side. A middle-aged man was carefully twirling a book rack, studying the paperbacks with a look of pure concentration. A bargain hunter.

Lisa made her excuses to the woman behind the

counter, cutting the conversation short. She hurried out of the shop and climbed into the car. It was 12.21. Time to go to Anniesland for her caring caller appointment with Annette.

As she drove off, she checked the rearview mirror.

How am I doing Tommy?

"I love your flat," Lisa said.

This was no hollow compliment. Annette's ground floor flat was in much better condition than Lisa's upmarket three-bedroom home in Kelvindale. The surfaces were spotless. The living room projected an effortless warmth. Lisa liked how the walls were covered in a variety of landscape paintings, most notably a framed replica of Constable's *The Hay Wain* that took pride of place on the living room wall. Lisa recalled a print of the very same painting in her gran's house back in the day. She'd grown to love that painting, its depiction of a pleasant summer's day in the English countryside. One look at the brilliant image on Annette's wall and Lisa was back in a safe place from her childhood. It was a good sign.

They were sipping green tea in the living room. On the mahogany coffee table, a plate of assorted biscuits was on offer.

"Thank you dear," Annette said, blushing slightly. Her voice was high-pitched, almost childlike. "I like my wee flat too. Help yourself to biscuits by the way – as many as you want. You could do with a wee bit of fattening up if you don't mind my saying so."

Lisa sank into the velvet brown armchair. She smiled at Annette, sitting on the other side of the mahogany table on a matching chair. There was no couch in the room. Just single chairs.

"No. I don't mind."

Upon arriving at the flat, Lisa had found Annette dressed in layers of heavy clothing even though it was warm inside and the heating was up full blast. After turning down the radiators, Lisa suggested they find something more suitable for Annette to wear. Annette agreed and they went to the bedroom where they found a pretty cream-coloured blouse hanging up in the antique wardrobe. Whilst searching for the blouse, they'd also found a beautiful silk shawl that caught Lisa's eye. That was when Annette opened up, telling Lisa that she'd bought the shawl in India whilst on holiday with her now deceased husband, Fraser. The conversation flowed after that. Annette seemed to take to Lisa and visibly relaxed in her company. Now, after barely an hour in the flat, Lisa felt like she was talking to an old friend.

The caring caller staff had informed Lisa about Annette's diagnosis prior to this first visit. The old woman was showing early signs of dementia. It had impaired her memory and she was prone to repeating some things as Lisa would no doubt find out. The trick, Lisa was told, was to smile and pretend like it was the first time she'd heard it. Do that and it was smooth sailing.

"You need a bit of fattening up," Annette said, watching Lisa cut two slices of the chocolate cake she'd brought with her.

Lisa handed a slice of cake to Annette. She took the smaller slice for herself and pointed her fork at the plate.

"I'll start with this then, shall I?"

It was a relaxed, enjoyable session that went better than Lisa had imagined. The two women spent the latter part of the afternoon browsing through Annette's photo albums. The first album covered the trip to India with Fraser, a man that Annette clearly still worshipped and adored. She pointed out the silk shawl whenever it appeared in those well-worn images. "There it is!" More albums came out. Lisa learned about Annette's life as a primary school teacher down in the Borders. She saw pictures of Annette and Fraser's only child, Samantha, who'd died in a car crash in her early twenties. Fraser had been a handsome, photogenic man. In his prime, Lisa thought, he bore a slight resemblance to Roger Moore.

"I miss them all," Annette said, snapping the final album shut. She spoke in a matter-of-fact voice but Lisa had already spotted the old woman's eyes welling up as she gently placed the final album at the top of the pile with a sigh. "I didn't expect to miss them so much. I didn't think it was possible."

"It must be hard," Lisa said.

"I didn't expect to outlive my daughter. That's for sure."

"You've been through a lot. Haven't you?"

"Haven't we all?"

Lisa nodded and stared down into the empty teacup in her hand. "My husband, Tommy. He died."

Annette's face creased with sympathy. Her voice shot up a register as she stood up, walked slowly around the table and grabbed Lisa's forearm. "What happened?"

"He drowned. Don't worry, this was over a year ago."

Annette maintained a surprisingly strong grip on Lisa's arm. "You miss him badly, don't you?"

"I do."

"Of course you do," Annette said, letting go of Lisa at last. She backed away towards her seat. "Well, I don't know about you pet, but I take comfort in knowing that my Fraser's still with me. He is, you know? He's with me."

She put a hand over her heart. Sat back down in the velvet chair.

"How about you Lisa? Do you ever feel like your husband – what did you say his name was again love?"

"Tommy."

"Do you think Tommy's still with you?"

Lisa shivered as a cold draught seeped into the room and then rushed down the back of her neck.

"Yes," she said. "I think he's still around."

13

Lisa sent Malcolm another text, asking if he'd be okay with her taking another week off work. One more, she said. That's all and then she'd be ready to get back into the swing of things. Malcolm replied, saying he was only too happy to see Lisa, a workaholic for most of her life, take some well-earned time off.

He also asked Lisa about the coffee and chat. Lisa typed out a swift response, letting him know she'd be in touch. A minor delay, she said, nothing more.

That same day, Lisa took Annette for a walk in Dawsholm Park. They walked through the woodlands, enjoying the sound of the birds in the trees. The sun was out and it felt wonderful to be a little closer to nature. There were dogs everywhere, many of them bounding over to say hello to Lisa and Annette before running back to their people with their tails wagging. The two women strolled alongside the River Kelvin at a leisurely pace, talking here and there in between long, comfortable silences. Neither one was in any particular hurry to get back to their homes.

Following the walk, they stopped off for coffee and cake in a small, family run café next to Glasgow University. They sat outside under the awning, digging their forks into cake and watching the world go by.

The past few days had been quiet. There were no more letters on the doorstep or phone calls waking Lisa up in the middle of the night. No sightings of Tommy. Was that it? Whenever the thought came up, Lisa told herself that she shouldn't dare to hope. It was foolish to hope and yet that's exactly what she was doing.

Was it over?

She'd given away money, clothes, time and she was even scheduled to give blood the following week. What else could she do to make it up to him?

"Are you okay?" Annette asked. Her voice was miles away.

"Sorry," Lisa said, blinking hard. "I was just thinking... oh, I was daydreaming. That's all."

Annette wiped the corner of her mouth with a napkin. "And they say it's *my* mind that's going."

Lisa had to laugh. "What can I say? It's been a tough couple of weeks." She glanced at the steady flow of human traffic walking past their table. There were a lot of people out and about. Blank faces carrying reusable shopping bags, rucksacks, briefcases. Most of them looking at their phones. Everyone looked busy apart from Lisa and Annette.

"I'm fine," Lisa said, getting back to Annette's question. "Better than fine."

Annette cut off a corner of the half-eaten brownie on her plate. The fork worked slowly and methodically. "Are you still moving? That *was* you that said you were moving, wasn't it?"

Lisa nodded. "It's time. There's too many memories here."

"Aww," Annette said, sitting back, her jaw moving from side to side as she chewed. She waited until the food was down before continuing. "I'll miss you love. I know we haven't known each other for long but I'll miss our wee chats. It's been nice talking to someone who would've been my Samantha's age. Made me feel like, well, made me feel like I had a daughter again."

That last part hit Lisa hard. She wanted to tell Annette that being around her was like having a mother again. And there was something else, something that Lisa didn't get elsewhere. Everyone wanted something from her except Annette. Her friends could never know what she did that day in the river and so Lisa had been pushing them away for months. And they kept pushing back. Kept calling. She could never hope to relax around them again.

All she had was this wonderful old lady who was slowly losing her mind.

"I'll miss you too."

"Aye."

"But listen," Lisa said, leaning forward and tapping a finger off the table. "I don't want you to worry about having someone to talk to when I'm gone. I'm going to recommend a couple of my friends to the agency. Deb and Risha. They're lovely people and they're always talking about doing something like this. You'll like them."

"Ach, don't worry about me Lisa. It's you I'm worried about. To lose your husband at such a young age, I can only imagine what it's been like for you. At least I had my Fraser till he was in his seventies."

Lisa picked up her coffee. She felt the sun touch her face and leaned into it. "It's been tough."

Annette frowned. "What did you say his name was again?"

"Tommy."

"Aye," Annette said. "That's it. Tommy. Well, take my advice love – one day at a time, that's the best you can do. It's the only thing you can do. Move forward at your own pace and don't let anyone else force you into doing anything too fast. Grief is different for everyone."

Annette lowered her voice a notch.

"That's what grieving is. One step at a time. Getting through the next second, the next minute, the next hour. You feel okay. Then you feel like the world is collapsing around you. But with each step, it does get easier to bear. You might never get over it but you learn to live with it. To carry it."

Lisa gave Annette's hand a gentle squeeze. There was so much familiarity between them that she wondered if she knew this woman in a previous incarnation.

Wow, she thought. Reincarnation. If Deb could only hear me now.

"So," Annette said, propping her elbows on the table. "Where are you going to move to? What takes your fancy?"

"Down south, maybe."

"England?"

"It's a possibility," Lisa said with a shrug. "Lots of opportunities down there, I'll say that much for it. Having said that, I've always fancied going over to Ireland."

Annette smiled. "That would be lovely. Like you say, depends on the opportunities available, eh?"

"Exactly."

Lisa thought about all the research and networking that lay ahead of her. And how little she'd done so far.

"Well," Annette said, placing her empty coffee cup on

the saucer. She pushed it back a little across the table. "Anyone would be lucky to have you. It's just nice to see you smiling honey."

The old woman laughed and cut into the last of the brownie.

Lisa *was* smiling more today. She could also feel her appetite coming back and for the first time in a long time, there was no desire to lose herself inside a bottle of Pinot Gris. The walk in the park and the sunshine had revived her. No letters, no phone calls and no sightings of Tommy – that had revived her too. A cruel weight was sliding off her shoulders at last. She had the will and energy to start laying the groundwork for those big changes. Today, not tomorrow. She'd do it today.

Lisa spent a productive night on the couch, doing research on the MacBook with a movie playing in the background. It was an old seventies movie, one in which Al Pacino's character tried to rob a bank to fund a sex change. As you do. It was more Tommy's kind of thing, one of those gritty seventies flicks with Pacino, De Niro, Keitel or whoever. But it was nice to have something on, even if she wasn't paying much attention to it.

After a couple of hours researching veterinary practices in the UK and Ireland, Lisa composed a draft email of an introductory letter. She laid her soul bare in the letter. Kept it honest, relaying how the decision to move had been triggered by personal loss. She hoped that any potential bosses out there would appreciate her honesty. If she was lucky, they'd relate to it and it might spark a connection. Lisa didn't mind working for someone else after being a co-owner for so many years. In fact, she was happy to do it. To have less responsibility. She also updated her neglected LinkedIn profile, adding a more flattering but slightly outdated photo. Her CV there got a makeover too.

There was a cup of tea on the table. An empty plate with a faint trail of pasta sauce running over it. The sleeping pills were in the drawer upstairs but after a busy day, Lisa felt tired enough to go to sleep without them. She was hoping for a solid eight hours tonight.

After working a little longer, Lisa turned off the TV and the downstairs lights. She checked the locks, then went to bed early, climbing under the sheets at nine o'clock on the dot. Her alarm was set for five o'clock. The plan was to get up, go to the gym (renewing her membership was something else she'd accomplished that evening) then get to work on stuff for the move. Tidying the house was on the list. Also, pouring all the wine down the sink and getting rid of the alcohol.

The sleeping pills, they could go too.

Lisa slept for the intended eight hours with no interruption. She woke up with the alarm, refreshed and energetic. She took a few minutes to wake up, browsing Facebook on her phone for the first time in months. Nothing much going on there. Afterwards, she got up, washed her face, brushed her teeth and tied her hair back. Hurrying downstairs, Lisa checked the gym bag that she'd packed last night to make sure she had everything she needed. After a quick cup of tea and a banana for fuel, she walked through the hall, grabbed the gym bag and pulled the front door open.

The envelope was sitting on the doormat.

MaKe iT uP To mE

Lisa dropped the bag on the floor.

She stared at the envelope for what felt like hours. The top corner had been partially tucked under the doormat to prevent it from blowing away.

It wasn't over, she thought. And deep down, despite the optimism, you knew it. Just because she'd had a few good days. Done a good deed or two. It meant nothing. Lisa sat down on the floor, toying with the possibility that she was doing this to herself. That in some guilt-induced blackout, she was typing out the letters, sealing them up and leaving them on the front step. Why not? It was obvious she was losing her mind, wasn't it?

Lisa stood up.

She picked up the A4-sized envelope, peeled it open and pulled out the sheet of typewritten paper inside. What now? Was Tommy going to ask her to help dyslexic children with their homework? Ask her to become a lollipop lady? To volunteer in an animal sanctuary?

What the fuck did he want?

Lisa's eyes skimmed the text. Not quite believing the words, she read it again. And then again. After the third readthrough, Lisa was ready to throw up the tea and banana breakfast. This letter was different from the others.

Random Acts of Kindness, Part 4 - SPREAD THE LOVE

Provide comfort to those who are less privileged. Go find homeless people in the city centre and beyond. This time you don't have to give them money. Give them time. Share a drink, feed them, talk to them nicely. Buy them clothes if they need it.

Then give them your body.

Fuck them.

If you don't, everyone will know what you did under the water.

Fuck them all.

Watching you.

Tommy

Lisa hadn't cried in months. But now it came suddenly, the dam bursting open at last.

14

Lisa didn't hear the car pull up outside the house. Didn't hear the brisk footsteps marching up the garden path. There was only a brief knock and when Lisa looked up, Deb was standing in the open doorway. Hands on hips. Staring across the hallway at her weeping friend sitting on the stairs.

"Lisa," she said, a shocked look on her face. "What's wrong? I knew I'd catch you if I came over at this time of day. Look at you. You've lost so much weight and you're as white as a sheet. And you're crying for God's sake."

Lisa wiped the tears off her face. "Hi Deb."

Deb closed the door behind her. There was a cautious glance down the hallway, as if she wanted to confirm to herself that they were alone in the house. Deb was a tall woman, 5'11 in flats, in her late thirties and with a pretty face she always covered with makeup. Her blonde hair was loose and wavy. She wore a summery dress covered in flowers. Looked to Lisa like she was ready for a day of modelling at the beach.

"What the hell's going on with you?" Deb said, nudging Lisa aside and making room on the bottom step.

"You don't answer calls. You're ignoring texts. I know you're getting my texts by the way. And I know you know I know."

Lisa spoke. It felt like something sharp was caught in her throat. "Something's happening to me Deb."

Deb glanced at the piece of paper in Lisa's hand. "Lisa, you can tell me anything. You know that, right?"

"I know."

"This something that's happening to you. It's related to the anniversary, correct? Risha told me the memorial was hard for you."

Lisa's head flopped onto Deb's shoulder. She closed her eyes and wondered what she'd be doing if she'd gone to the gym as planned. Treadmill? Kettlebells? Maybe a swim in the pool. She missed the gym – her body missed the gym and so did her mind. "I can't take it anymore."

"Take what? You miss Tommy that much?"

"No, it's not that."

"Then what is it? Lisa, I'm so confused sweetie. We just want to help you get through this, whatever *this* is."

Lisa lifted her head off Deb's shoulder. Wiped her eyes again, then let out a deep sigh that sounded like a dying breath. "You won't believe me if I tell you."

Deb's booming laugh made the house tremble.

"What's so funny?" Lisa asked, frowning.

"Oh my," Deb said, her laughter trailing off. "Have you been avoiding me so long you've forgotten who you're talking to here? It's Mystic Meg for God's sake. I'm the woo-woo queen, remember? And that's a nickname you gave me by the way – you and Risha, the rational-minded scientists of our gang. What on God's earth would little closed-minded Lisa Granger believe that I wouldn't?"

Lisa offered Deb the letter. "You asked for it."

Deb glanced at the A4 sheet. Then at Lisa. "Asked for what?"

"I think Tommy's back."

Deb's head jolted backwards. She snatched the letter out of Lisa's hand and read, her lips silently tracing the words. "What the flipping...what in the name of God is this nonsense?"

"I've been getting letters like that for a while," Lisa said. "From someone claiming to be Tommy. That's the fourth one, I think."

"Tell me you're kidding. Tell me this is a joke."

"What do you think?"

"Please Lisa."

Lisa shook her head. "It's not a joke Deb. And it's not just the letters either. I've...I've seen him."

"Tommy?"

"Yes."

"Where?"

He was in a car park in Edinburgh and it *was* him before you start giving me any crap. This was after he'd called me in the room. I spoke to him. Then he was at the bottom of the street one day, just out there."

Deb whistled softly. She stared at the letter again, narrowing her eyes. "Okay, I can't believe I'm going to be the sceptical one but here goes. It's a prank. I've told you about these kinds of people before, remember?"

"Yes, but..."

"Trolls. Ghouls – whatever you want to call them. They're real, they're out there and they're messing with your head."

"I don't think so Deb. I wish that was true but..."

"This is despicable," Deb said, cutting Lisa off. "It's disgusting but it's classic ghoul behaviour from these sickos.

Do you really think that Tommy would ask you to do something like that? I mean, what the hell? Spread the love? Ughhh, oh my God. This letter was written by someone who wants to humiliate you. Tommy loved you. He adored you. Why would Tommy want to hurt you like this?"

Lisa gripped the edge of the wooden staircase, squeezing down till her knuckles turned white.

"Because he's angry with me."

"What? Why is he angry with you?"

"Because I wasn't there for him."

Deb made a loud scoffing noise. Then she slipped her arm around Lisa's shoulder. "Pardon my French darling, but that's fucking bullshit and you know it. I told you – didn't we have a conversation about these weirdos? They're sad, lonely people. Men, of course. They scour newspapers and websites looking for accidents and deaths. They see something they like and get all excited. Probably gets them hard, that's if they can get it up at all. They mark the dates on their calendars, wait for the anniversaries to roll around and then start trolling the mourners when they're still vulnerable but more clear-headed than they would be immediately after the death of their loved ones. Honestly, it gives me the creeps. Praying upon a widow like that. Call the police. Get them on the case. I can call them if you like. I'll do it right now."

Deb reached inside her bag for her phone.

"No," Lisa said, pulling Deb's hand out of the bag. "I don't want you to do that."

"Lisa, this is twisted."

"It's not a troll. I saw him Deb. I saw Tommy."

Deb turned her attention back to the letter. She reread the demands and sighed. "Maybe you saw someone who looks like Tommy. Hmmm? The trolls – sometimes they go to extraordinary lengths to mess with people. There are articles about it. There was a documentary on BBC One. They'll dress up. Dye their hair, you know? Do whatever it takes to get noticed."

"I think I'm going crazy," Lisa said.

"You are *not* going crazy. There's only room for one crazy person in this friendship and it's not you."

Lisa took the note out of Deb's hand. "I need to ask you something."

"Shoot."

"Tommy drowned," Lisa said, her voice dropping to a whisper. "That's a horrible way to go. He wasn't ready to die, you know? When he was under there, you know, his emotional state heightened and with so much racing through his mind, is there a chance that some part of Tommy could..."

"Survive death?"

"Yes."

Deb's answer was swift. "Yes, there is a chance."

"Do you really believe that Deb?"

"I believe it *can* happen," Deb said. "But I don't think it's happening here. I don't believe Tommy is writing these letters to punish you for not being there at the end. That's a classic guilt response. You blame yourself for not being there."

"Why couldn't Tommy come back?"

"Tommy died," Deb said, her voice taking on a mournful tone. Her eyes welled up. "He died Lisa. They pulled his body out of the river and Iris identified her son. There was a funeral and he's gone. And I really believe that he *is* gone. You know me Lisa, if I thought there was a chance that Tommy was still around then I'd say..."

"But he suffered so much."

"How do you know that?"

"It's obvious, isn't it? Is drowning peacefully even a thing?"

"We don't know for sure what happened," Deb said, shaking her head. She wasn't looking Lisa in the eye anymore. "Maybe he was knocked out when the car hit the water. Maybe he hit his head off the wheel and..."

"He wasn't driving," Lisa said.

Deb cursed under her breath. "Sorry."

There it is, Lisa thought. That part of Tommy's death that nobody, not even her two best friends, liked talking about. The pregnant girl in the driver's seat. It was so much easier for everyone to stick to the sad story of Tommy the angel and forget about the girl. Forget about what really happened. And what it meant.

"Lisa," Deb said. "Take my word for it. This whole thing is a sick prank. It's nothing more than that, I promise."

Lisa shook her head. "It's more than that."

"It's not. It's someone with nothing better to do than torment vulnerable people. I can't believe you of all people are talking like this. How many times have you ridiculed me when I've talked about spirits and the departed? Look, you might be carrying some guilt because you weren't there but I do know this – you're the last person in the world who's responsible for Tommy's death."

"Deb..."

"What do the other letters say?" Deb asked. "Are they as bad as this?"

"Nothing's as bad as this."

"I still think you need to go to the police," Deb said. "This person needs to be caught as soon as possible or who knows how bad it'll get. Dressing up like Tommy, is he?

What if that's just for starters? What if he tries to get into the house while you're here?"

"There's something else," Lisa said. "Something I haven't told you yet."

Deb's eyes narrowed with apprehension. "Good lord. Okay, I'm listening."

"They know things. Things about me that only Tommy knows. Like an old nickname. And something else we used to say to each other that was between us. You don't even know these things, Deb. How's a random troll going to find out?"

Deb didn't seem fazed.

"You'd be surprised what the good ones can find out. Watch that BBC documentary. I'll send you the link if you want. They can find out anything Lisa. *Anything*. Especially in this day and age. These trolls, they're skilled detectives. They deep dive into social media and go after everything and everyone. They find contacts. Approach those contacts to gather information, pretending it's for something else. Has anyone asked you for money yet?"

"I've donated to charity."

"A real charity?"

Lisa nodded.

"It's not Tommy," Deb said. "Get it into your head and keep it there. I know you want him to be alive but he's not. He's gone."

"I have to know that for sure," Lisa said. "I have to know for sure that he's dead the way you say he is. When I find that out for sure, I'll accept that it might be a high-level ghoul waging war against my sanity."

"How can I help?" Deb asked. "Just tell me what you need."

Lisa's face was grim. "Is there someone that you trust.

Someone in your magic circle or whatever who can tell me for sure."

Deb laughed. "Good lord in heaven. I never thought I'd see the day that Lisa Granger asked me for a psychic. You must be desperate."

"I'm as desperate as they come."

Deb sighed, then stood up. She took a few laboured steps across the hallway. Then she turned back to Lisa.

"There is someone."

"Who?"

"I've seen her just once. She's barely more than a girl. Twenty-one or twenty-two, something like that. But in terms of consistency, she never gets it wrong. Never. Now, I'll give you fair warning. This one's a bit of a livewire and whatever you do, don't call her a psychic to her face. She hates this stuff as much as you do but she's good at it. That means you'll need to pay her well."

Lisa couldn't believe she was talking about this stuff with Deb and taking it seriously. But she was out of options.

"All I want to know is, can she tell me? Can she tell me if Tommy's still around?"

"Yes," Deb said. "I know she can."

"And you trust her?"

Deb leaned her back against the front door. "Okay. Let's put it this way. I wouldn't trust this girl to look after my cat if I was going on holiday for two weeks. I wouldn't trust her to look after my cat for two hours. But for this sort of thing, she'd be my first port of call in an emergency. What's more she'll give you a straight answer. Whether you like it or not."

Lisa glanced at the note.

Spread the love.

"Okay," she said, getting to her feet. "Where do I find this girl?"

15

Lisa walked into King Tut's Wah-Wah Hut on Saturday afternoon, a little after three o'clock.

King Tut's was a live music venue in the city centre. It was a grungy, down to earth club with rundown wooden tables and brightly coloured glass bottles and candles sitting atop the bar. It wasn't Lisa's scene, that much was clear from the get-go. She'd never been much of a gig-goer but like many others, she'd heard of King Tut's and knew about the venue's stellar reputation. That reputation dated back to the early nineties, not just locally but nationally. Blur, Manic Street Preachers and other famous bands had all played Tut's at some point. Oasis had been discovered there in the early nineties.

Lisa made the short walk through the front bar to the upstairs area where the music stuff took place. Gigs, she corrected herself. She couldn't call it music stuff in front of anyone in here or she'd be laughed out of the building. There was already a soundcheck underway. Someone was hitting a bass drum, kicking out a stamping, monotonous rhythm that gave the building a shudder-inducing heartbeat.

There were more wooden tables and chairs scattered around upstairs. A tiny bar to the left. The stage and sound desk off to the right.

Lisa felt like a fish out of water. Scruffy musician types littered the area, hanging around in their little tribes. Dyed hair, ripped clothes, sullen expressions. Lisa tentatively approached the stage as if walking the plank. There was a bald guy with a long pigtail beard standing behind the desk, pushing buttons, turning dials or whatever these tech people did. A heavyset, bearded drummer in a Nirvana vest top was alone on stage, sitting behind the kit. He was hitting a different drum at the pigtail man's request. There was a slightly bored look on a face riddled with piercings.

The drum was so loud that Lisa thought her head might explode.

She was distracted from the noise when two people shot out of nowhere, almost knocking her off her feet. They were engaged in a ferocious shoving match, one that was steering its way from the stage towards the bar. It was a blatant mismatch in terms of size. A small punk rocker woman was pushing back a giant of a man with a massive red mohawk that almost scraped the ceiling. The woman was little more than 5'5 at most, dressed in a black singlet and tight black jeans. Her arms were covered in ink: Celtic cross tattoos, dragons and other lavish designs that Lisa didn't understand. She rammed her spiky, green pixie haircut, shaved at the sides, towards the man's face like a pair of antlers.

"You ever touch my fucking bass again," she said, a ferocious snarl on her face, "and I'll cut your balls off with a dull blade. You hear me?"

"I never touched your bass," the big mohawk said, hands up in the air. "I was just having a look at the paint job."

The girl shoved him back a few steps. She was stronger than she looked.

"Having a look? I walked in and saw you touching it with your manky fingers. I don't know where your hands have been, do I? You ever hear of asking?"

The mohawk groaned. "Aw, fuck off ya mad boot."

Behind Lisa, the drummer was still working his way through the drums while pigtail beard behind the desk adjusted the levels. Lisa was more focused on the argument, which by now had drawn a few amused glances from the sidelines. In particular, Lisa was staring at the green-haired tornado.

That was Deb's girl. It had to be.

"Fucking ask next time you want to touch my bass, alright?"

Mohawk guy sidestepped the woman, angling towards the stairs. He saw Lisa and rolled his eyes in embarrassment.

"I'm going for a shite," he declared to the whole room. He hurried downstairs, calling back one last time. "Never touched your poxy bass by the way."

The green-haired woman stood at the top of the stairs, hands clamped to her hips, staring the mohawk down till he was out of sight.

"Keep walking prick."

Deb's description was accurate. Green hair, small, feisty. Pretty and savage. You'll know her when you see her.

The punk girl glared at Lisa for a second, then stormed over to the bar with a face like thunder. Lisa followed at a close distance. The girl leaned over the bar, waving towards a twenty-something barman with a thin moustache that looked like it had been sketched on with a pencil. The barman, writing something on a clipboard, signalled to the girl that he'd be over in a minute.

"Fuck's sake," the girl hissed.

Lisa made her way slowly towards the bar. As she did, she glanced at the posters on the wall advertising an upcoming punk rock night. Old school punk. *Not diluted. Not for the faint-hearted.* A quick check of the date told Lisa that this was tonight's entertainment.

She inched closer to the girl. Onstage, the drummer was soundchecking the hi-hat and cymbals. It was quieter now and Lisa knew this was the best time to make herself heard over the racket.

"Excuse me."

The girl turned around, sizing Lisa up. Then she looked away, uninterested.

"Are you Quinn Hart?"

"Depends who's asking."

"What?"

"Does Quinn Hart owe you money?"

Lisa shook her head. "No. I've got a job for her."

The girl's attention drifted back towards Lisa. She offered her hand.

"I'm Quinn Hart."

"My name's Lisa Granger," Lisa said, taking the outstretched hand. The green-haired woman had a sturdy grip. "I'm here because my friend Deb arranged a meeting with you. I'm a little early, sorry about that."

Quinn nodded. "I take it you're the woman with the husband problem."

"That's one way of putting it."

Lisa pointed to the stage. "Can we talk somewhere else? Have you done your...?"

"Soundcheck?"

"Yes."

"Aye it's done. I was just dealing with that cheeky bastard from Smashed Jackson touching my bass right after I'd tuned it. Nerve of the prick. It's sabotage if you ask me. Messing around with another band's instruments, trying to knock them out of tune. Just 'cos his band is shite."

Lisa listened, a polite smile on her face. "Can we talk then?"

"Aye," Quinn said, turning back towards the bar. "We'll go downstairs in a minute where it's quiet. I'm just trying to blag a drink off this wee twat behind the bar. Look at him pretending to write on that clipboard."

Lisa rummaged around inside her bag. She found her purse. "I'll buy the drinks downstairs."

"That bar doesn't open till four o'clock. They won't serve us and neither will this one. Until then, we survive on our wits and charm."

Quinn slammed the counter with her hand. "Hey pal! I don't bite."

The barman lowered his clipboard and walked over. Lips pursed, shaking his head. "Aye? What is it?"

Quinn held two fingers up. Like she was flashing the peace sign. "Two beers, eh?"

"This bar's closed for drinks pal," the barman said. There was a curt nod towards the stairs. "Downstairs opens in about half an hour."

"I'm in one of the bands," Quinn said, leaning so far over the counter that she was almost levitating. "I'm playing here tonight."

The bartender shrugged. "Where's the rest of your band?"

Quinn didn't miss a beat. "Gone for food. Probably

because everyone's so tight around here they won't give us something to eat."

"Cannae get you a drink either."

"Take it off the rider."

The barman snorted with laughter. It was an awkward response and his face hurried back into a bland scowl. "Rider? What rider's that pal? Is Paul McCartney playing here tonight or something?"

"Why are you being a dick about it?" Quinn said. "Just give us a couple of cans out the fridge man. We've sold a shitload of tickets for tonight, aye? I'm in Blood Sandwich. We've sold more tickets than all the other bands combined. Least you lot can do is shout me a complimentary beer or two."

"Bar's closed."

The barman turned around and went back to stocking the fridge. Quinn stayed put, elbows propped up on the counter. Staring at his back. Lisa waited a few minutes and was about to tap Quinn on the shoulder when one of the tech guys called the barman over to the stage. The barman hurried away, a slightly worried look on his face.

He left his post unguarded.

Quinn watched him go. She looked at Lisa, pressed a finger to her lips. When the barman was front of stage, she took a leisurely walk behind the bar and grabbed two Budweiser bottles out of the fridge. She returned to the counter, pulled the lids off both and then crept back to Lisa with a satisfied grin.

"Now we can talk."

Lisa pointed to the bottles. "Won't you get in trouble for that?"

"For what?" Quinn said, heading towards the stairs. "Nothing to see here. C'mon, I don't have all day."

She led the way downstairs, picking out a table near the front door. As they sat down, Quinn slid one of the beers in front of Lisa.

"Cheers."

"Thanks," Lisa said, grabbing the icy cold bottle neck. She didn't like Budweiser but she wasn't going to say anything after Quinn had gone to the trouble of securing them a drink.

She took a sip. Stole a glance at the girl across the table.

Quinn was attractive in an offbeat kind of way. She didn't wear much makeup. Her skin was so white that Lisa didn't know if she was using some kind of goth cream or whatever those tortured-looking people used to achieve the vampire look. She had a small mouth, a labret stud gleaming under her bottom lip. Piercing blue eyes. The sort of eyes that didn't miss much.

Quinn swirled the beer around in her mouth like it was mouthwash. Then she swallowed. At least half the Bud was gone already.

"Thirsty?" Lisa asked.

"Always."

Quinn dried her lips, wiping the back of her hand across them in a sawing motion. "So what do you want?"

"You spoke to Deb, didn't you?"

"I don't know Deb," Quinn answered. "Deb spoke to a mutual contact of ours, a woman called Marie, who sometimes finds me *this* kind of work. I got a brief rundown of your situation but I forgot the specifics. No offence."

"So you're a musician *and* a psychic?" Lisa asked.

Lisa immediately regretted using the 'P' word, recalling Deb's instructions not to do so. Deb had even repeated those same instructions last night on the phone. The word 'psychic' was out of bounds. Do. Not. Use. It. This girl,

Quinn Hart, wanted nothing to do with that kind of labelling.

"I'm a bass player," Quinn said. "That's all you need to know about me."

"But you have these abilities."

"Listen..."

"I'm sorry," Lisa said, cutting the young woman off. "But I don't know if I even believe in any of this. You're charging a lot of money for your services and I have questions."

A short pause. Both women took a sip of beer at the same time.

"You don't have to believe in something for it to work," Quinn said. "Hell, I don't even know what I believe and yet here we both are."

Quinn looked at Lisa and shrugged.

"Fair enough. Shoot. Ask whatever you want."

"Is it clairvoyance?" Lisa asked.

"Been on Google, have we?"

"Maybe."

"Nah. Clairvoyance is seeing. What I do, it's more like clairaudient. I don't see anything. I hear it. I feel it. Using the sensory information provided, I can join the dots together. I'm good at joining the dots. At pulling a story out of chaos."

"It's strong? This thing you have."

"That's an understatement. What did you say your name was again?"

"Lisa."

"Lisa, that's the understatement of the century. It's a flood of noise. Let me put it this way – imagine the worst group of musicians you ever heard jamming a song you hate inside your head. Okay? Every single instrument is a mile out of tune and they're all playing out of time. Turn that up by a hundred. Then you're scratching at the door."

"Is it bothering you now?" Lisa asked.

"I have ways of suppressing it. It's either that or the loony bin."

"How?"

Quinn flicked her finger off the bottle neck. The Bud rang like a tiny bell. "With this. Alcohol. Smoking. Other drugs. If I keep up a regular intake, the door stays closed. If I lay off it for too long, the door squeaks open."

"Wow. That's..."

"You don't believe me, do you?" Quinn said, laughing. "You think I'm full of shit."

"I don't know what I believe," Lisa said.

Quinn glanced around the room. Then she picked up her bottle and drank the last of her beer.

"Back when I was younger," she said, "it was just this rush of noise shooting through my head. Like some kind of acid-tinged tinnitus. Imagine the worst headache you've ever had, throw in a bunch of scary shit on top, images and voices, and then try and make sense of it with a child's mind. It's not happening, right? But as I got older, things *did* make more sense. It was like learning a new language. After some familiarity with that new language, I got better at putting the big picture together."

"You didn't always have it then?"

"No."

"What happened?"

"What do you want? A biography? Do you ask the plumber for his life story every time he comes over to fix the toilet?"

"Sorry. Just curious."

Quinn finished her beer and glared at the bottle. Resenting its emptiness. "Listen, I only do this sort of work when I'm broke. Flat broke. Right now, I've got a lot of fucking debt hanging over my head and it's making my life a misery. I've been paying double rent for three months since my turd of a flatmate walked out on me with zero notice. Honestly, I can't bear the thought of finding a new one. The landlord hates me because it's always a day or two late. Big deal, eh? Bitch is a walking talking headache."

Lisa listened carefully. "You're not like any psychic I've ever met before."

Shit, she thought. There was the 'P' word again. Fortunately, Quinn didn't react.

"Have you encountered many?"

"No."

"Then how do you know what they're like? Were you expecting the old lady in the fairground with the warts and crystal ball?"

"I suppose."

Quinn pointed at Lisa's beer. The bottle was still at least three-quarters full. "Are you driving?"

"Actually, I am. You want the rest of it?"

Quinn grabbed the beer. Tapped a finger off her head in salute. "Cheers."

She took a drink and then glanced at Lisa.

"You rich?"

"No. Why do you ask?"

"Because everyone else in here is dirt poor and you stick out like a sore thumb. Still, you're rich enough to pay me what I want, right?"

Lisa couldn't help but think that Quinn was taunting her. The warts and crystal ball type would have at least been familiar.

"There's a group at my local library," she said to Quinn. "They're young people, late teens probably. They have these meetings on Wednesday nights where they sit around and hear from people trying to reach their loved ones. Their dead loved ones, that is."

Quinn gagged, pretending to throw up. "They're full of it."

"It's free. They don't make any money."

"It's free but I bet they get lots of attention, right? And they get to feel important?"

"Won't be seeing you there anytime soon then?" Lisa asked.

Quinn smiled.

"Trust me," she said, tapping a finger off the side of her head. "If the library gang had this, they'd be just like me. You understand? I don't celebrate it or push it except when I have bills to pay. And I have a lot of bills to pay right now."

Lisa's voice was quiet. "Can you help me?"

Quinn fussed a little over her hair. She leaned back in her seat, sipping the beer and staring at Lisa. "What do you need?"

Lisa felt some resistance. But she had to get comfortable with saying it out loud. "I need you to tell me if my husband's really dead."

"You don't think he is?"

"I don't know anymore. Things have happened. Strange things that I don't understand."

Quinn chewed on her bottom lip for a while. "I can do that. I can tell you if he's dead and if there's anything else. Any trace of him that's come back."

"Like a ghost?"

"That's one way of putting it."

"Just like that?" Lisa asked.

"Well, I have to go through hell first. But sure, just like that."

"How does it work?"

"Just think of me as a radio tuning into different frequencies. Aye? That's the best way I can put it."

Lisa flinched as the soundchecking band upstairs broke into a raucous punk rock number. The floor pulsed to the beat. The empty Bud bottle on the table began to tremble. Lisa leaned over the table, raised her voice a notch in order to be heard.

"How do I know you're not full of shit? No offence but Deb's a much more open-minded person than I am. Especially when it comes to all this."

"You don't know," Quinn said. "But if you don't like it, *no offence*, you can fuck off to the library and hold hands with the virgin club. It's all the same to me."

Lisa nodded. "Deb said you were different."

Quinn touched her ear. "What?"

"DIFFERENT. Deb said you were different."

"That's one word for it."

"She also said you were the real deal. And that's why I'm here. Because I trust her and quite frankly, I'm desperate."

"I get it," Quinn said.

She finished the second beer and stood up. Looked to Lisa like the girl was about to walk off. Instead, she came over and leaned into Lisa's ear.

"In order to do this," Quinn said, "I have to stay clean for forty-eight hours. I don't drink, I don't take drugs. I don't fuck. No weed, nothing. I limit sleep to four hours a night because being sleepy seems to help. I eat very little and whatever I eat is clean. I drink only water. After those forty-eight hours are up, I'm as pure as a virgin's kiss."

"I hope so," Lisa said.

Quinn straightened up, took a step back towards the stairs. "Only one way to find out Neo. You're going to have to take the red pill."

Lisa stood up, offered her hand.

"I'll do it."

Quinn stared at Lisa's outstretched hand. There was a flicker of distrust in her eyes. "You'll pay what I ask? Half before, half after?"

"Yes."

Quinn shook Lisa's hand. The little punk's grip was once again formidable.

"Next week Alice," she said. "Let's see if we can't bring you back some answers from Wonderland."

16

On Wednesday morning, Lisa opened the door after a mostly sleepless night. Quinn was standing on the doorstep, dressed in a plain black t-shirt, ripped jeans and a pair of Doc Martens that added an extra couple of inches of height.

"Morning boss."

"How was the gig?" Lisa asked, standing aside to let Quinn into the house.

"Shite," Quinn replied in a hoarse voice. She walked in, examining the sparse hallway with a mildly amused expression. "The sound guy was atrocious. Off his head on pills before the first band had even finished their set. My ears are still ringing."

"Sorry to hear that."

"No biggie. No one asked for their money back."

Quinn re-examined the surroundings in more detail. "This is a nice house. I should be charging more for my services."

"Good one," Lisa said. "You were charging plenty last time I looked."

"True. But a good tip is always appreciated."

"I'll bear that in mind."

Lisa stood in the hallway, feeling awkward. She wished that Deb was here for moral support. This sort of thing was her territory, not Lisa's. What was supposed to happen next? Did she take the lead or leave it the girl? Offer Quinn a drink? Water, of course.

"You're clean?" she asked, as if it was something they had to get out of the way. "You're not on anything?"

Quinn gave a curt nod. "Clean as a newborn baby's conscience. Three days. Sunday. Monday. Tuesday. Nothing but water and a little unprocessed food. Four hours sleep a night, mostly. I feel like shit but that means I'm match fit. On the bright side, my bank account looks better. Thanks for the advance."

Lisa nodded. "How's the head?"

"Don't ask."

"Do you want a glass of water?" Lisa asked, pointing her thumb towards the kitchen. "I can get you..."

"Nah," Quinn said. She searched out the living room and walked in, beckoning Lisa to follow. "Let's just get on with it, shall we?"

Lisa followed Quinn into the living room. "How did you get here?"

"Bus."

"From?"

"City centre. I live in a flat on Hill Street, near the art school."

"That's nice."

"Uh-huh."

They stood in the centre of the living room. The house was quiet and even outside, all the usual early morning sounds of the street were absent. There was no distant buzz of daytime traffic. The birds in the garden had taken a break from chirping, almost as if they knew something was going on in the Granger house. The house itself wasn't too messy. Instead of tidying up properly, Lisa had thrown most of the crap into drawers and wardrobes and although it was a temporary fix, it was a start. She'd sprayed lemon air freshener and yet the smell of stale smoke persisted.

Lisa shrugged. "What now?"

"Can I see the letters?" Quinn asked.

Lisa had gathered the letters whilst cleaning up, placing them on the inside shelf of the coffee table. She scooped them out, handed them to Quinn.

"That's all of them."

Quinn read the letters in chronological order. "Shit," she said, handing them back. "Was your husband a big charity guy or something?"

"Not really. No more so than the average person."

"Was he a voyeur?" Quinn asked. "Into kinky shit? Did he ever watch you having sex with anyone else? Or express an interest in it?"

Lisa was taken aback. "No, of course not."

"Well," Quinn said, pointing to the letters in Lisa's hand. "That's the first time I've read those and the overall vibe is that the person writing the letters wants you to become a more charitable person. They also want you to do some extreme sex stuff. But it's not about the charity or the sex. It's about humiliating you. Most of all, it's about hurting you. Someone out there really doesn't like you."

"Good work detective. Deb said the same thing."

Quinn ignored the quip. She continued to stare at the letters. "What makes you think your husband wants to humiliate you?"

The words tripped over Lisa's tongue on their way out.

"I...I don't know. Look, all I need to know is whether Tommy's dead and gone. Or if there's something still here."

Quinn stared at Lisa. Lisa felt like a suspect in a brightly lit interrogation room.

"I get that," Quinn said. "But if he didn't die, why would he be out to get you? Why would he want to hurt you? Did you two hate each other or something?"

"No."

"Okay. Marriage is weird."

Lisa felt like she'd said too much already. "Can we just get on with it?"

"Alright," Quinn said, her eyes narrowing. Clearly, she knew that Lisa was holding something crucial back. But Lisa hoped the girl was only interested in money and would stop asking so many questions.

"First up," Quinn said. "I need an object. Is there something in the house that was dear to Tommy? It can be anything. An item of clothing. A photograph. A book. Something that he was particularly attached to?"

"What for?"

"Big word of the day time," Quinn said. "Psychometry. Gleaning information through physical contact with an object. Making associations. Simply put, I hold the object and shit comes through my head in the form of sensations. Noise. There's a story somewhere in that noise. If I dig through the weeds, I'll find that story and it might tell me something about the fate of the owner."

Lisa felt like throwing up. "I just want to know if he's dead. That's all I need to know. Is Tommy dead and gone?"

"Still think you're being ripped off?" Quinn asked.

"What?"

"You don't look very convinced."

"I don't know," Lisa said with a shake of the head. "I

don't know anything anymore. I don't even know if I still want to go through with this."

"Look," Quinn said, her tone softening a little. "This stuff might sound like bullshit and believe me, I wish it was. My life would be so much easier. Just remember though, whenever you feel silly, that the CIA used psychics for years. And they weren't the only ones."

"I thought you didn't like the 'P' word."

"True, but it has its uses. Now, do you have that object?"

"I think so," Lisa said.

"Go get it for me, will you?"

"Right."

Lisa walked upstairs, dragging her legs like she had heavy weights attached at the ankles. She went into the spare room, which was always warm and pleasant in the morning light. She stood by the bookshelves, studying Tommy's books. Kneeling down to access the lower shelves, Lisa pulled out the tattered hardback copy of *The Giant Nature Encyclopaedia*. It was a brick of a book. A lethal weapon. It was also Tommy's childhood favourite, handed down from his paternal grandmother, a woman he'd only known for a short time before dementia took her. There was a handwritten dedication inside, a messy scribble of blue ink from Granny Granger to Tommy and his sisters telling them how much she loved them. Lisa had often found Tommy sitting on the bed, thumbing through the well-worn pages, staring at images of orcas and sharks and massive coral reefs. No wonder he used to make Lisa sit through those hour-long BBC or National Geographic documentaries about marine life and complex ecosystems. Tommy couldn't get enough of that stuff. And it all started with this book.

Lisa held the book to her chest. She closed her eyes, saw

the big screens at Tommy's memorial. Images of a gorgeous curly-haired boy chasing after a football that was almost the same size as him.

She opened her eyes, half-expecting to see the adult Tommy sitting on the bed. Reaching for the book in her hands.

Drip, drip, drip.

Lisa hurried downstairs. Back in the living room, she handed it over to Quinn.

"He loved this."

Quinn studied the ancient cover, a plain green background with faded gold text. She opened it up, read the dedication and smiled. "This'll work."

"What do you want me to do?" Lisa asked.

"Nothing. Just sit on the couch, take the phone off the hook and switch your mobile off too while you're at it. No interruptions, okay? That'll mess up everything. Don't move and try not to freak out, no matter what you see. This won't take long."

"What?" Lisa said. "What am I going to see?"

"Just sit down and keep it zipped."

Quinn lowered herself onto the jute rug on the living room floor. She crossed her legs, gripping the book on her lap with both hands. Lisa watched, still feeling unsure about all of this. Looked like Quinn was about to bless the house. Or rid it of a demon.

Quinn's breathing began to slow. As it slowed down it became more pronounced.

Lisa sat down after taking the landline off the hook. She shivered, as if the room had grown colder.

Quinn sat perfectly still for five minutes. Sitting and breathing. Five minutes that felt like an hour as far as Lisa was concerned. She watched in silence from the edge of the couch, trying to silence the inner cynic that warned her she was watching an actor at work. A con artist, one bleeding her out of a grand for absolutely nothing. A grand for God's sake! What was she thinking?

Nonetheless, there was a crumb of comfort in her suspicion. If Quinn didn't have psychic abilities, she couldn't discover things that Lisa didn't want her to know. That she didn't want anyone to know. God, this was stupid. It was a bad idea. But the alternative was to do what the fourth letter told her to do.

Spread the love.

Quinn frowned, registering some discomfort. Deep lines grooved her forehead. Lisa felt another cold shiver as she watched the girl's fingers twitch. *Fake, it's fake*. Then Quinn's arms flopped to the sides. She was no longer in contact with Tommy's book, which fell onto the mat. To Lisa's horror, Quinn began to claw at the floor. The sound of fingernails scratching the jute rug filled the living room.

A loud gasp.

Quinn tilted her neck back. It was a sudden, eerie manoeuvre. Stiff and robotic. There was a throaty, gargling noise that made Lisa's throat tighten just listening to it. Sounded like what she'd heard on the phone during those Tommy calls. Someone struggling to breath. *What the hell is going on?* Her jaw hit the floor as Quinn lifted her arms and began to windmill them in the air. Lisa didn't understand. She went to the rational thoughts first. Told herself that Quinn was a conwoman overdoing the theatrics. She *had* to be a conwoman.

Deep down, Lisa knew better. Quinn wasn't windmilling for effect. She was hitting something with her closed fists. And now with her elbows.

Something like a car window.

Lisa couldn't watch anymore. She fell back into the couch and covered her eyes with her hands. She had no idea how much time passed before she heard Quinn breathing heavily on the floor. When she opened her eyes, Lisa saw a look of muted terror on the young woman's face. An avalanche of sweat gushed down her forehead. Looked like she'd just tried to sprint a marathon.

"Quinn?" Lisa whispered. "Is it over?"

"Can you get me a glass of water?"

"Sure."

Lisa jumped off the couch and hurried to the kitchen. She brought back a glass and the Brita jug. She poured a drink for Quinn who devoured it like she'd just spent a week lost in the Sahara. Lisa poured a second glass and Quinn took care of it just as quickly.

"Are you okay?" Lisa asked.

Quinn's first response was to pick up Tommy's book and toss it across the room like a frisbee. The book's flight was short-lived. It skidded off the floor before crashing to a stop against the legs of the dining table.

She grunted in disgust. "I don't ever want to see that again."

Quinn laboured back to her feet. Rubbed her temples as if trying to prise something loose under the surface. "Shit, shit, shit."

"What happened?" Lisa asked.

Quinn's chest continued to heave up and down as she stared at Lisa through bloodshot eyes. Eyes that were somehow different. "Can I ask you a question"

"Yes."

"Were you there?"

"What?"

"Were you in the water with him?"

Lisa felt like she'd been punched in the face. She couldn't say anything. It felt like her tongue was crippled.

Quinn gave Lisa that probing cop look again. "I couldn't make sense of it at first. But I felt the water filling my lungs. I felt the fear of someone drowning. Then there was something else. Confusion. A sense of..."

"What?" Lisa asked.

"I'm not sure. If I had to put it out there, I'd say it was betrayal."

Lisa swallowed hard. "Betrayal?"

"Earlier on," Quinn said, lowering herself onto the couch, "you hinted that Tommy might be angry with you. But you didn't say why. He was looking at something or someone under the water. Tommy's focus wasn't on escape, it was on something else. Something happened down there. He was surprised. Shocked. Someone he knew was in the water and it had to be more than the people he was with. It was someone he didn't expect to see. Was it you?"

"I..."

"But you weren't in the car," Quinn said. "Were you?"

Lisa felt like her feet were sinking into the floor.

"No, I wasn't."

"Were you following him?"

"No."

"Hey," Quinn said, hands up in the air as if Lisa had just pulled a revolver on her. "Listen up, okay? I'm not the police. I'm not judge, jury or priest either. Quite frankly Lisa, as long as your money's good my lips are sealed. Client confidentiality, eh? I'm just trying to put the pieces together here because this is a strange one and that's saying something when it comes to this kind of thing. You weren't in the car. You weren't following him. So what the hell?"

Lisa dropped onto the couch beside Quinn. “I *was* in the water.”

Quinn nodded. “That much I’d gathered. So what happened?”

“He kept cheating on me,” Lisa said. “Tommy was a good man but he had a weakness for younger women. We’d been fighting for weeks but he wouldn’t admit that he was doing it again. I’d been trying to get it out of him. A confession. I just wanted to hear him say the words. To see the look on his face. That day, it was like the universe threw me a bone. I was out walking off a hangover and it slapped me in the face with the sight of a speeding car plunging into the river. I dove in. There was Tommy in the car with his twenty-year-old slut.”

Quinn poured herself another glass of water. “I felt my lungs filling up with the river. I felt fear. And yet, there was hope. An outpouring of love. And then, the confusion and betrayal.”

“Because I swam away.”

“Why was Tommy in Clydebank with the girl?” Quinn asked.

“Who knows? A quickie in the backseat by the river? One of his workmates, Alec, has a flat in Clydebank or nearby. There’s every chance Tommy has a spare key to Alec’s flat and well, you know what men are like. They’ve got each other’s backs.”

“Takes guts to dive into the river like that,” Quinn said. “Not sure I’d have done it.”

“I’m a pretty good swimmer.”

Quinn shrugged. “So am I.”

“Well,” Lisa said. “Hopefully you’ll never have to find out.”

Quinn put her glass down on the table. She wiped

another layer of sweat off her brow and fell back onto the cushions. "So, you made the decision to leave him after you saw them together?"

Lisa stared at her feet. "You think I'm a monster, don't you?"

"I don't know you," Quinn said. "But all things considered, I wouldn't say you're a monster."

"No?"

"But you didn't save him either," Quinn said. "That's cold."

Lisa stood up, unable to sit still.

"He was cheating on me. *Again*. Making a fool of me. *Again*. I couldn't give him a baby so he went looking elsewhere and found Abbey Donaldson with her long legs and tight arse. I'm sorry for the baby, I really am. The only innocent victim in this whole mess. But Abbey was unconscious when the car went under. I don't think she knew what was happening. As for Tommy, he could've got out if he wanted to. He didn't realise that the door would open once the car was below the surface."

Quinn nodded. "Lack of oxygen will do that."

Lisa felt dizzy. She leaned her legs against the side of the couch and waited for it to pass. "You haven't told me yet."

"Told you what?"

"What I'm paying you to tell me."

"He's dead," Quinn said. "Totally dead."

"But what does that mean?" Lisa asked, sitting back down. She filled Quinn's glass with water from the jug and took a drink herself. "The letters, the phone calls, the sightings – what does it mean?"

Quinn stole a glance around the living room. "There's nothing of Tommy in this place. Only objects, like that book. He's not writing those letters."

"That's impossible," Lisa said. "It has to be him."

Quinn picked at the upholstery on the couch. "Hey, you got any beer or wine or joints? My head's killing me, you know? It's hard to concentrate on what you're saying."

"There's always wine here," Lisa said.

"Sounds good."

"I'll get it."

"Quick," Quinn said, wincing and grabbing the side of her head as if she was planning to pull a chunk off. "Please."

Lisa hurried to the kitchen and came back with an unopened bottle of Pinot Noir. She unscrewed the lid, poured two glasses and Quinn drained hers in a matter of seconds. The young woman grabbed the bottle and poured herself a second.

"Don't mind me."

"Help yourself."

Lisa sat down, staring at the floor. Her eyes narrowed in concentration. "I was thinking about something Deb told me. About these trolls. Ghouls, she calls them. I'm talking about the sort of people who get their kicks tormenting the relatives of dead people."

The colour was seeping back into Quinn's cheeks. After a third glass of wine, her eyes were bright blue again. "There are some sick fucks out there."

"Could this be something like that?"

"Why not? It's not your dead husband coming back for revenge."

"You're drinking yourself into an early grave," Lisa said, watching as Quinn poured glass number four. "My grandfather was an alcoholic and it wasn't a pretty sight in the end. Hospital. Tubes sticking out of him everywhere. The yellow skin. Your liver won't thank you for this in the end."

"The sooner the better," Quinn said. "Think I want to live to a hundred with this shit in my head?"

"I don't understand."

Quinn sighed. She put the glass down and stared across the room.

"My head's been a king-sized disaster since I was six. I'm twenty-two now. That's a long time to put up with shit."

"What happened to you?" Lisa asked, turning towards Quinn. "If you don't mind my asking."

Quinn hesitated. She was picking at the upholstery again.

"My mother was murdered."

"Oh God," Lisa said, raising a hand to her mouth. "That's...that's terrible. When?"

"I was six."

"Jesus."

"I remember it quite vividly," Quinn said, sitting with her hands tightly clasped together. "It happened at home. I was sitting on the floor one morning, playing with my toys and watching cartoons. Mum was sitting in the armchair, about a metre and a half away. We heard a loud bang. That was the front door being kicked open. To me, it sounded like a giant landing on our roof."

Lisa tried to imagine Quinn as a six-year-old child underneath the green hair and attitude. It wasn't easy.

"This big fucker thundered into the living room," Quinn said, "carrying this sledgehammer like it was a pencil. He didn't speak. Didn't say a word. He swung the sledgehammer and bludgeoned Mum as she blocked the route to me. I just sat there, watching as he turned her head to pulp."

"The Hammer killings," Lisa said. "Right?"

"Right."

"I remember them well."

Quinn nodded. "That's when the noise started. I didn't hear it until a few weeks later when I was living with my grandparents. Some would say it's a response to grief. Shock-induced trauma. A malfunction. A gift or a curse. Either way, it happened. But what good is it when this Hammer prick walked away? They never caught him."

"I can't imagine," Lisa said. "To have witnessed something like that at six years old. I'm so sorry."

Quinn sat on the couch, poker-faced. Seemingly unmoved by the recollection of her mother's murder.

"Do you regret what you did?" she asked Lisa. "Leaving him down there?"

"Yes."

Quinn nodded. "I regret not helping Mum. I regret not screaming. Not making enough noise to alert the neighbours in time. Maybe I couldn't help her but I might have been able to get enough people over to catch the evil fucker."

"You were a child for God's sake," Lisa said. "What happened to you afterwards? Did you go to school? To college?"

"Bailed out of school early, did odd jobs and ended up drifting my way back to Glasgow at seventeen. Got some paying gigs as a musician, did a bit of teaching. And when I'm really desperate, I put myself through *this* shit."

The two women shared a brief silence. Outside, Lisa could hear the birds chirping again. The sound of voices on the street.

"Am I crazy Quinn?" Lisa asked. "These letters, I mean. What if I'm doing this to myself? What if there's some kind of mental dissociation at work and I'm typing these letters in a deluded state?"

"I had thought of that."

"And?"

Quinn laughed. "Can I make a suggestion?"

"What's that?"

"You're way too emotionally involved in all this to be the one doing the detective work. You're being targeted by someone. That's stressful as hell. It's no wonder you haven't cracked the case yet."

"Do you have any better ideas?"

"As a matter of fact," Quinn said, grinning from ear to ear. "I've got two. First of all, you need an objective eye working on this. A hired gun, if you like. You can't go to the police, I understand that. But there are others out there, people who are discreet. Put them onto this. That'll take the pressure off you. Secondly, you need to shift your focus away from Tommy."

Lisa frowned. "What else am I supposed to focus on?"

"It's obvious, isn't it?"

"Apparently not."

"The girl in the passenger seat," Quinn said, her eyes clear and focused. "What did you say her name was?"

"Abbey Donaldson."

"What about *her* family? That's where you need to go next. Someone in her inner circle must have known what was going on with her and Tommy. About the baby too. She didn't keep that to herself, I'll bet money on it."

"I don't know much about Abbey."

"Where's she from?"

"She used to be part of a traveller community in Newton Mearns," Lisa said. "But she left them to move into a flat share, not far from here. She was going to college or uni or something higher education like that."

Quinn stroked the tip of her chin. "Travellers in Newton Mearns? That must be the Stewarton Road site, right?"

"You know it?"

"I know it. There's this obnoxious gobshite called Donnie who lives there. He sells some of the best weed in the city."

"Why are you asking me about Abbey's family?" Lisa asked.

Quinn stood up, grabbed Lisa's arm and pulled her up to her feet. "Let's get some fresh air, eh? How about you show me where Tommy's car went in the water?"

Lisa was repulsed at the thought of going back to the crash site. She pointed to the bottle on the table. "I've had wine. Don't know if I can drive."

"Bullshit. You've barely had a glass."

Thirty minutes later, Lisa and Quinn were in Clydebank. Standing at the exact spot where Tommy's car had gone into the water. It was tame in comparison to the horrific memory that thrived in Lisa's imagination. She had distorted so much about the crash site over the past year. It was a pleasant spot. Quiet and peaceful. Somewhere to pull over and look across the water if the mood hit you. The flimsy wire fence that had allowed Tommy's Audi to go into the river was gone. The steel barrier was whole again and most likely had been for the better part of a year. There was no way that sort of crash could happen again. Not unless they invented flying cars.

"Why are we here?" Lisa asked.

Quinn's answer was brief and to the point. "I wanted to see it."

"Do you feel anything?"

"I just guzzled half a bottle of red wine at your place. If anything, I feel a little sick. Kinda hungry too."

"I haven't been back here since it happened," Lisa said.

Lisa noticed Quinn threading a guitar pick through her

fingers. Staring at the water with a look of total concentration.

"Why are we here Quinn?"

"For the conclusion of today's visit," Quinn answered. "And here it is – Tommy's gone. He's dead and buried. Your husband isn't the one tormenting you, Lisa. That's just the guilt."

"I know," Lisa whispered. "Deb said the same thing. But there are so many questions still unanswered. What am I supposed to do next?"

Quinn tapped her on the shoulder. "You hire me all over again."

Lisa tilted her head. "You? But you're a..."

"You don't need a psychic anymore," Quinn said, cutting in. "You need a good old-fashioned private investigator to do the legwork for you. You need someone to get out there, asking the right questions to the right people. Do that and you'll start getting somewhere."

"Why you?" Lisa said. "Why are you the right person to do this?"

"Because I'm good at joining the dots. Whether it's the noise in my head or the noise out there, I'm your best chance at solving this puzzle."

Lisa sighed. It was a long time before she turned back to the river.

"This is going to be expensive, isn't it?"

PART 2 - QUINN

17

The travellers' site was located in a car park seven miles southwest of the city centre.

As Quinn approached, she tried to recall the last time she'd visited the Stewarton Road camp. Almost a year ago? She'd arrived late with a group of piss-drunk revellers after a hellacious thrash metal gig at the Barrowlands. It was a flying visit with the sole purpose of scoring weed and at the time, it had been too dark for Quinn to remember much about the site – the layout, the people, whatever. Not that she'd been paying much attention at the time. Now it was broad daylight and the car park was full of people wandering around outside the caravans going about their morning business. Dogs barked. Kids played football, tag and other games. The sound of eighties rock music spilled through an open window somewhere.

There were several rows of caravans neatly parked, stretching from one end of the car park to the other. Some of the vans weren't too shabby either, Quinn noticed. Some of the better ones reminded her of the big fancy trailers used on a Hollywood film set. Not what she'd been expecting.

She walked slowly, overhearing snippets of conversation. The people onsite greeted her cordially enough but Quinn saw the caution in their eyes. The wariness. She was a stranger after all.

Perhaps they saw a fellow outsider.

Quinn had no idea if Donnie still lived here. If he didn't, her only contact in Abbey Donaldson's world was a dud. There was no Plan B either. She'd found Donnie's number in her old phone listed under 'Donnie – pikey weed dealer from the Barras'. She'd called the number ahead of her visit to Newton Mearns today but it rang out. Texts weren't delivering either. Quinn was beginning to think that Donnie had moved on. The travellers had been on the Stewarton Road site a long time and it was inevitable that some of them would have left Glasgow by now.

"Help you love?"

A tall woman approached Quinn with a friendly smile. She was about fifty and dressed in a grey, closed cardigan and black jeans. Her wrists were covered in layers of shiny bangles and she had matching earrings, like miniature hula hoops hanging off the sides of her head.

"I'm looking for a guy called Donnie," Quinn said. "Don't know his last name but he was staying here last time I heard."

The woman's face didn't lack expression. Her eyes widened. There was a mischievous grin stretching from ear to ear. "Oh aye. And what do you want with Donnie?"

"Umm..."

"Looking for something to smoke, are you?"

"Smoke?"

"Aye," the woman said, clearly pleased with herself.

"You're looking for something to smoke. Some wacky baccy. Nothing to be ashamed of my darling." She jerked her thumb towards the back of the car park. "Over there. He's in that little banger."

The woman turned around, cupped her hands over her mouth.

"DONNIE!"

A moment later, the hinges on the door of one of the older vans groaned. The door opened from the inside.

"DONNIE!"

"I'm coming for fuck's sake!"

A short, chubby man, wearing pale blue jeans and a white vest shirt, poked his head through the narrow doorway. He stepped outside, recoiling slightly from the daylight as if it might turn him to ash. He shielded his eyes with one hand, the other scratching at his ample belly.

"Margaret, was that you screaming my name?"

"Someone to see you Donnie," the woman said. 'A pretty little visitor."

Donnie left the van and walked over in Quinn's direction. Then he stopped, his eyes lighting up when he got a proper look at her.

"I remember you."

He smiled and even from afar, Quinn saw the gaps in his teeth. The sight triggered memories of a drunken Donnie trying to get it on with Quinn in the Barrowlands that night last year. She recalled his efforts to stick his tongue down her throat and how he'd tried to persuade her to go home with him. The stink of vodka and tobacco on his skin. She'd had to play nice that night because she and her mates wanted Donnie's weed. After getting what they needed, they ran out on him.

Now she was back.

"What are you doing here?" he asked.

"Alright Donnie?" she said, closing the gap.

Donnie stared at Quinn through narrow, slit-like eyes. He pointed at her. "That green hair was silver last time I saw it, eh? Shorter too."

"Good memory," Quinn said, grinning. Her hair had been red. It had also been longer last year. Donnie didn't need to know that.

"I don't forget the wee things."

"So I see," Quinn said.

"What do you need?"

Donnie's accent was from the east, Quinn observed. She vaguely remembered him saying something about Dunfermline. About Fife. But he'd been in Glasgow for a while. As long as anyone in the camp so he must have known about Abbey.

"Just trying to score a wee bit of weed, eh? My usual guy's out of town and I remembered you down here. I tried calling the number you gave me last year. Tried texting but guess it's out of date, eh?"

"I change numbers a lot," Donnie said. He lowered his voice, looked back and forth as if he thought the FBI were somehow watching him. "It's safer that way."

"Fair enough," Quinn said.

Donnie's face melted into a wide, toothy grin. "You're the bass player, eh? Still playing music?"

"Aye. It's tough though."

Donnie grinned. "Ye no famous yet?"

"Fucking megastar mate," Quinn said, a hint of impatience creeping into her voice. "Limo's waiting just down the road there. You see it? Don't all the celebs come out here for their weed?"

Donnie's husky laugh filled the car park. He took a step

closer, his eyes running over Quinn's body. She tensed up. Saw that the big man fancied himself as a regular old George Clooney. Nightmare, she thought. But she had to ride this out. She wasn't here on personal business and that meant she had to soak up Donnie's cringey behaviour no matter what he pulled. Within reason, of course. But if she wanted to learn more about Abbey Donaldson, the girl who drove Tommy Granger's car into the Clyde, Quinn was going to have to put on her big girl pants.

Donnie led her towards the beat-up caravan at the back of the car park. "What took you so long to come and see me?"

Quinn's polite smile was starting to wear thin. "I was coming up here to score last year but then I heard..."

She hesitated. Too soon?

"Heard what?"

"About that car crash in Clydebank. The pregnant girl. Turned out she came from here, didn't she?"

Donnie bit down on his lower lip. "Oh aye. Wee Abbey – that was a shocker."

"Figured you guys had other things on your mind at the time," Quinn said. "So, I stayed away. Out of respect and that."

Donnie nodded. "Abbey had moved on from this place anyway. She was living in a flat in the west end when it happened. A posh student flat in Kelvindale no less, ye believe that? She was going to college, trying to better herself. She was still one of us though. Still family."

For a moment, Donnie looked lost. It was as if the weight of her death had hit him all over again.

"Tell you what though," he said, shielding his eyes from the sun. "It's a bloody shame what happened to her."

"Aye," Quinn said. "It was."

Donnie stopped at the door of his caravan. He turned back to look at the surroundings. "This camp got a lot smaller after it happened, that's for sure. Abbey's people cleared out, including her folks. So did a few others."

He whistled softly, then grabbed the door handle. "Anyway. Ye up for a wee smoke before you head off? Better sample the merchandise before you buy, eh?"

Merchandise, Quinn thought. Fat fucker thinks he's Tony Montana.

She nodded. "Aye, I'm in no rush."

Quinn didn't want to go anywhere near Donnie's caravan. It looked like an old vintage job from the seventies or eighties. Retro, that was the kindest way of putting it. The old thing was badly in need of a makeover. The exterior was grimy and worn, including the tow hitch and tyres. Damn thing didn't look roadworthy.

Donnie pushed the door open and the hinges made that loud groaning noise again. He led her inside the van. Quinn's nostrils would have sealed up if only human evolution had made that a possibility. The reek of stale smoke combined with alcohol and a thousand rotten curries was horrendous. There was a dining area to the right where a rundown couch encircled a badly chipped table. The table was drowning in beer cans, cigarette packets and junk food wrappers. A metal ashtray that looked like a giant dog bowl spilled over with ash and cigarette butts. To the left of the main door, a narrow corridor sliced through a dump of a kitchen leading towards the bedroom and bathroom areas. Quinn didn't want to visit Donnie's bathroom anytime soon.

She'd heard about old vintage vans like this one having asbestos problems. It wasn't the sort of place she wanted to hang around for too long.

"Excuse the mess," Donnie said, gesturing for Quinn to

sit down at the table. "Wasn't expecting company, eh? Would've cleaned up a bit."

"It's cool," Quinn said, sliding along the couch. She put her back up against the window. A window she'd have to open if she wanted to breathe fresh air.

"Want a beer?"

"Aye."

Donnie pulled the fridge door open. He pulled out two cans of Heineken, walked over the tiled floor and sat down at the table. Grinning at Quinn, he slid a beer over to her.

"Cheers," Quinn said, pulling the tab on the Heineken.

"Cheers doll."

Quinn poured the beer down her neck. It was warm and flat. Of course it was.

Donnie slurped his beer and then, whistling a chirpy melody, reached for the Rizla packet next to the ashtray. He pulled out the skins, licked the edges and went to work building a joint.

"Two minutes pal," he said. "Best joint you've ever smoked, coming right up."

Quinn didn't want to talk about weed. She wanted to start probing Donnie about Abbey and finding out what he knew about her. But she had to be patient. This private investigating lark was new to Quinn but she knew enough about playing the long game. Patience, patience, patience. That was the mantra. Exercise the mantra. That meant letting Donnie's tongue loosen up with beer and joints. Then Quinn would start working him over. Finding out what he knew.

They smoked and drank, making small talk for the next half-hour. Donnie banged on about cars and football mostly, two things that Quinn didn't give a shit about. But she let him talk to his heart's content and feigned interested in every word. At the tender age of twenty-two, she'd built up a solid resistance to the effects of weed and alcohol and could drink most people under the table. She was fine, but Donnie was getting more wasted by the second. His cheeks were glowing. Eyes glazing over.

They were on their fourth can when the caravan door opened from outside.

"Donnie?"

A young woman, late teens or early twenties, marched up the steps. She was chewing gum and when she saw Quinn she stopped dead in the doorway. After a moment, she turned back to Donnie.

"Ye busy?"

"Frannie!" Donnie said with stoned excitement. "How's it going mate? Up for a wee smoke?"

The young woman glanced at Quinn. Then back to Donnie.

"Want me to go?"

Donnie burst out laughing. He got up and pulled Fran into the caravan, closing the door behind her. "Nah, you're alright. Quinn's an old mate. She's just sampling the merchandise before making a purchase."

He was slurring his words.

Shhamplin the merssshandishhhe before making a purchassshe.

Quinn smiled at Fran. If nothing else, it was a relief to have someone else inside the little shithole on wheels. Even if that someone was looking at Quinn like she was a piece of roadkill propped up on her favourite chair.

"This is Fran Buckley," Donnie said, gesturing towards the newcomer. "Fran was best mates with Abbey, the girl who died in that car crash. Those two lassies were inseparable, so they were. *Inshheppparable.* So inseparable that Fran went to stay with Abbey in her posh flat in Kelvindale, eh? Too good for the likes of the rest of us. That's Fran and Abbey."

"Fuck off Donnie," Fran said, taking a seat in between Quinn and Donnie. "How much have you smoked already?"

Donnie's glazed happy face was all the answer she needed.

"You shared a flat with Abbey?" Quinn asked.

Fran chewed aggressively on her gum. She blew a bubble that swelled to an impressive size until it made a loud pop. "Aye."

"I was just saying to Donnie," Quinn said. "Sucks what happened to her."

"Aye."

Fran removed the chewing gum from her mouth and wrapped it up inside an empty Curly Wurly packet on the table. "How about a wee blast of that joint, eh Donnie?"

"Aye. Sure."

Donnie relit the joint and passed it over.

Fran inhaled, blowing a fat cloud of smoke across the living room.

Quinn sat there, sipping her Heineken as Donnie and Fran caught up briefly. She watched the girl. Fran was about nineteen or twenty tops. She had a bright shock of Scandinavian yellow hair that ran loose down her back. Her physique was doll-like. Tiny hips. Narrow shoulders. The girl was so skinny that Quinn could envision Fran's exposed ribs poking out from under the tight Primal Scream t-shirt she had on.

"Open the windows," Fran said to Donnie. "Will you? It's fucking stinking in here man. You ever hear of air freshener?"

Donnie mumbled something that Quinn couldn't understand. He stood up, pulling at his sticky white vest that had a fresh Heineken stain on it. He laughed to himself as he pulled the kitchen window open. "Happy now Frannie? You're always on at me in here to open the windows. Every time you're in my car too, it's roll down the window Donnie, eh?"

"Any sane person who'd smelled the inside of your car would say the same thing," Fran said. "I like the wind on my face when I'm in a car, big fucking deal."

"So do dogs."

"Shut it Donnie."

Donnie chuckled as he walked back down the aisle. He squeezed his ample frame in between the table and couch and scooped up his can. "Where you staying these days Quinn?"

"Here and there."

"Sounds like a traveller, eh Frannie? You should have been one of us Quinn."

"Nah," Quinn said. "I couldn't live the way you guys do. No offence – I just don't get why anybody would want to live in the middle of a car park."

Fran's steely eyes lingered on Quinn. She passed the joint back to Donnie. The big man took it off her, flicked the ash off the tip and missed the ashtray by a mile. He nodded in Fran's direction. "Fran and Abbey didn't want to live in a car park either. That's probably why they pissed off to *Kell-lvindaaale*."

Quinn looked at Fran. "Is that right?"

"As usual," Fran said, "Donnie's talking out his arse. Abbey needed me so I went to stay with her for a while. It was never a permanent move."

"Why did she need you?"

Donnie made a loud cuckoo noise. He twirled his index

finger at the side of his head "Abbey wasn't all there. No disrespect to her memory. Lovely lassie and all – she was just a few cyclists short of a full Tour de France."

"Shut the hell up Donnie," Fran snapped. "You want to respect her? Shut your big trap."

"She was wee bit unhinged that's all," Donnie said, clearly wounded by Fran's outburst. "No shame in it, eh? Mental health. Everyone's talking about mental health these days. All the cool kids are mad."

Quinn's ears pricked up. "What happened to her?"

Fran shook her head, urging Donnie to keep silent.

"It's only Quinn," Donnie said, the glazed smile back on his face. "Abbey had her problems, that's no secret anyway. Poor lassie tried to kill herself twice after she moved into that posh flat with her posh flatmates. Pills, both times. Maybe it was just a cry for help, who knows?"

"Abbey was dating someone," Fran said. "She was head over heels, said this guy was the one. But he was no good for her. He was non-committal, distant, and he was with someone else. But Abbey was a bit obsessive about her men. A *lot* obsessive. He kept pushing her away and then coming back, all apologetic and round it went. It was a vicious circle of rejection and it chipped away at her already fragile state of mind."

"I heard she was pregnant," Quinn said. "Was that right?"

Donnie grunted. "Aye. And the prick of a father didn't want to know. That was the last straw."

Quinn nodded. She felt the fresh air coming in through the kitchen window. It revived her a little. "Do you think she drove the car into the river on purpose then? A third suicide attempt?"

Fran picked up the joint in the ashtray and relit it. She

let the smoke fill her lungs and exhaled. "Don't know. Abbey had a thing for water. She told me once that if she could die anywhere it would be underwater. Said it was peaceful down there. Not like up here where everything hurt so bad."

"Doubt she had the manky Clyde in mind when she said that," Donnie added. "More like the Mediterranean, eh?"

A picture was starting to take shape in Quinn's mind. Abbey Donaldson was obsessed with a non-committal man who was in a relationship with someone else. That man had to be Tommy Granger. An affair had blossomed after they'd seen one another around Kelvindale. For Tommy, the affair was about sex. For Abbey, it was love. Then Abbey got pregnant and things grew complicated. Tommy panicked and being the lowlife scumbag he was, he didn't want to know. After that final big fight with Lisa, he'd tried to end it one morning. He'd been kind to Abbey. Shit, he'd even let her drive the fancy car. And yet none of it mattered. A heartbroken Abbey had hoped for a life with Tommy and their child. That was her dream and Tommy said no. She freaked out behind the wheel. Saw an opportunity for a beautiful water death with her man and baby beside her. The family, all drowning together.

Quinn felt a cold shiver run down her spine. "That's a sad story," she said to the others. "Poor girl."

Quinn caught Fran staring at her. Those narrow bird-like eyes burned with distrust.

"So you think you're too good to live in a car park?"

"I didn't say that," Quinn said. "I said I don't see the appeal."

"You don't see the appeal," Fran said, "because you don't have the history of the travellers flowing in your veins. Not like me. Not like Donnie and everyone else around here. If you did, you'd see the point."

"History?"

"Did you know this car park was built over the site of one our oldest camps?"

"No," Quinn answered.

"Well it was. Went back for generations. And that old camp was shut down years ago, just like that."

Fran clicked her fingers.

"And did you know that no one wants to reopen that camp either? They don't want to talk or try and understand our way of life. Fuck's sake man. It's a joke. There's so much tolerance for all kinds of people out there nowadays – black, brown, yellow and all those LGBT whatevers, but travellers? Forget it. The bastards build car parks over our old greens. We're pushed aside, left with nothing but concrete car parks to set up on. People have preconceived notions of what we're supposed to be. But we've been here for hundreds of years, all the families going way back. We've passed down stories and ballads. We've got roots and still we're treated like shite, just for existing. Just for being different."

"You'll have to excuse Fran," Donnie said to Quinn. "She's a bit of a crusader. Her old man's like that too."

Fran scowled at Donnie. "It's called fighting for freedom. Real freedom. The sort of freedom that scares the shit out of regular people."

"There she goes," Donnie said, breaking into a mock round of applause. "That's our Frannie. She'll be Prime Minister one day."

"You could try doing more for your people," Fran snapped. "Besides just getting wasted and dealing drugs."

Donnie was still laughing. "Hey! Don't get all Che fucking Guevara on me Frannie. You don't exactly come around here for my company, do you? Never seen you turn a joint down under this roof."

Quinn was eager to steer the conversation back to Abbey. But Fran was sitting up straight now, seemingly energised by the change in topic. Her feet were firmly planted on her imaginary soapbox. Quinn could just imagine Fran's old man preaching decades of injustice to his daughter over the years. Lighting a spark in her. Looked like most of old man Buckley's words had stuck.

"There's a shortage of legal stopping places," Fran said, smashing the last of the joint into the ashtray. "That's the problem. We set up in parks, greenbelt lands and industrial estates and it always causes tension with the locals. Every single time! The first thing they do when they find out we're here is to figure out a way to evict us."

"No wonder you're pissed off," Quinn said.

"Exactly. Listen, our way of life isn't for everyone. That's fine, you do you. But I don't like the idea of being stuck in one place. Of working a nine-to-five all my days. I want to live like my grandparents and my great grandparents before me."

"But you guys have been here in Newton Mearns for ages," Quinn said, glancing at both Fran and Donnie. "Thought you'd have moved on by now."

Fran took a sip of Donnie's beer. She grimaced and handed it back.

"Some of us couldn't leave after Abbey," she said. "Plus we've got a wee girl, Anne-Marie, who's unwell. She's registered with the local GP. Once she's better, the rest of us are gone. Maybe a few of us will stay."

"I'm definitely gone," Donnie said.

"Tinks. Pikeys. Gyppos," Fran said, the bitterness swirling around in her voice. "Some people just stick to calling us names. For others, it's organised racism. It's petitions to clear us off the land. It's a neverending battle and when you're fighting against the man all the time it's hard not to become resentful."

Quinn noticed that Donnie was on the brink of passing out. Fran, on the other hand, seemed limitless.

"We used to sell door to door," Fran said. "But they made it hard for us to get by like that. In theory, you need a licence. In practice, they make it impossible to get one. Metal recycling was a good earner for us. They've restricted that too."

"Sucks," Quinn said.

"Do you know what really sucks? Some of the people who rally against us go on to become big-time politicians in Holyrood. They sit in parliament for fuck's sake. What chance have we got against that? It's apartheid and it's happening right here in Scotland in the twenty-first century. We're being squeezed out of existence and the majority of the Scottish people don't know or don't give a shit."

There was a long silence. Quinn was more than ready to take the conversation back to Abbey.

"What was Abbey studying?" she asked.

"She wanted to be a teacher. Poor girl didn't realise that most people don't want their primary school teacher to be a traveller."

"Is that why she left here for Kelvindale?"

Fran shook her head. "She wanted to be closer to her man. Well, that and college."

She let out a long, tired sigh.

"Work. Education. Even private relationships. It's all fucked. Most people would be horrified if their son or daughter married into a traveller community. My boyfriend, thank God, he doesn't give a shit. I'm hoping he'll come with us when we leave."

Donnie opened his eyes. Blinked hard. "As you can see Quinn, Frannie's a right wee ray of sunshine."

Fran ignored his teasing this time. She turned back to Quinn.

"Abbey wasn't a perfect human being by any standards. And she might have liked to flirt with older men too much. But she died in that crash too and yet all the journalists wrote about was Tommy Granger. Poor Tommy Granger. Even his wife got more press than Abbey. How sad it was for her, being a widow and blah-blah. What about Abbey? They shoved her aside, even in death. Pregnant? Aye. But she was only a traveller. Just a wee pikey slag that let herself get knocked up."

Fran stood up and wiped a bead of sweat off her forehead. "I need to lay off the weed man. It's putting me on a right downer."

"No half," Donnie growled.

Fran backed off towards the door. Quinn edged forward on her seat, desperate for the skinny young woman to stay a little longer. There were several scenarios taking shape in her head now. She was starting to join dots and she needed Fran to help her complete the work. But it was too late. Fran was already gone. She slammed the caravan door shut without a word and Quinn heard her stagger down the steps, hurrying away from Donnie's caravan.

Quinn sighed. Fell back into the couch.

She looked over at Donnie. He was fast asleep across the table. Snoring like a big dog.

18

Quinn was back in Clydebank, standing at the exact spot where Tommy Granger's car had gone into the water. She looped the guitar pick through her fingers as her mind ran over the possibilities.

What the hell had she gotten herself into?

Staring down at the water, Quinn envisioned the car floating on the surface, bobbing up and down like a giant piece of litter before it sank. Had Abbey really driven the Audi into the water on purpose? Just the thought of it scared the shit out of Quinn. How far gone did anyone have to be to do such a thing? She ran over the scenario in her mind for the twentieth time. Lisa and Tommy argued the night before the crash. Lisa stayed at her friend's house and then walked to Clydebank first thing in the morning. That's when it happened. Had Tommy, following the final argument with Lisa, chosen his marriage over the affair with Abbey? Tommy was a prick but he wasn't stupid by all accounts. Had he called Abbey that night to arrange a dawn meeting before work?

Quinn wondered if Tommy knew about the pregnancy.

Nine weeks, that wasn't too far gone. She could only imagine how Abbey, already unstable following two suicide attempts, would take the news that Tommy was ending it.

And what about Lisa? Would she still have let Tommy drown if she knew that he'd chosen her?

Damn it, Quinn thought. What a mess. Too many questions, not enough answers. Tommy was a piece of shit for cheating on Lisa but did anyone deserve to watch their loved one swim away like that? That was cold. Quinn recalled the experience in Lisa's house. How she'd felt, albeit briefly, exactly what Tommy had felt at the end. It was the worst feeling ever. Standing at the river and staring at the water, that experience hit even harder. Tommy's death had been agony. It was like Quinn had captured an echo of that day, of the sheer terror he'd felt at the end. Worst of all, the horror of Lisa's abandonment.

"Jesus," she said.

She took a deep breath.

So, a crazy jilted and pregnant Abbey had driven the car into the water as an act of suicide? It was murder-suicide with Tommy in the car. Right? Not forgetting what was growing inside her. The murder-suicide theory was a good fit and yet Quinn struggled to accept it. And what about the letters? If she couldn't make sense of the car going into the water, what hope did she have of cracking the mystery of the letters?

She slipped the guitar pick into her pocket. Pulled out a cigarette and lit up.

"Tommy and Abbey," she said, staring across the water. "What were they doing in Clydebank?"

Why here of all places?

Quinn took the iPhone out of her back pocket. She heard a car horn blaring in the distance. Straight ahead, a helicopter on the other side of the river was travelling south in the direction of Glasgow Airport.

She felt like this case was slipping away from her. Joining the dots in her head was a lot easier than joining them on the outside. Why had she offered to take this on? Who the hell did she think she was to be charging Lisa for this shit?

With the cigarette hanging from her lips, Quinn googled the Granger car crash from last year. She threw in a bunch of keywords, *Clyde, Granger, crash, Abbey*. Then she searched for images. There was one image in particular that kept coming up. One she'd seen in almost all the news articles – a picture of the Grangers' white Audi as it was being hauled out of the water. Police standing around everywhere. Some of the articles had a small headshot of Tommy in the corner. Looked like a passport photo. Not a bad-looking guy with his funky blond curls and full lips. Still a dickhead though. Quinn had seen this picture several times since taking the case. She'd read the headlines too.

'TWO DEAD AS CAR PLUNGES INTO CLYDE'.

She browsed the meat of the stories. One thing was certain – Fran Buckley had every right to be pissed off about the way they treated Abbey in the press. The articles were fixated on Tommy and there was very little mention of Abbey in there considering that she'd died too. When she was mentioned, she was always qualified as a traveller. Some implied that she was a murderer.

Quinn shook her head. Tommy was a married man but according to the press, it was Abbey who was the slut. If anyone had a right to come back from the dead, she thought, it was Abbey, not Tommy.

The story had fizzled out quickly. Tommy wasn't a celebrity and as for Abbey, it was one less traveller in the world. Other news stories came along and pushed the crash out of the limelight. Soon it was just one more tragedy in the rearview mirror.

Quinn browsed through other images associated with the crash. She eventually found a shot that covered a different angle of the car as it was being dragged out the river. Pinching the screen to make it bigger, Quinn stared at the picture, hypnotised by every little detail. She zoned in on the front, then on the back half of the car. Stared at it for what felt like hours, not daring to blink.

She heard Donnie's voice in her head. It was playing on a loop – what he said about Fran and Abbey being inseparable.

The phone was so close to Quinn's face it was tickling her nose. And then she saw it, right there in front of her.

She gasped.

"I'll be damned."

Quinn thumbed out of Google Images. She navigated her way to her contacts as a hot rush of excitement shot through her body. The dots were starting to move – starting to join together. This was a breakthrough. It felt like she was about to walk onstage for the biggest gig of her life.

Lisa Granger. She had to call Lisa.

Tell her she knew who was writing those letters.

19

Quinn was sitting at the bar, picking restlessly at the label on the Peroni bottle. It was her first drink of the day and surprisingly for Quinn, she'd barely made a dent in it.

She'd scheduled a half-past two meeting with Lisa at Nice 'n' Sleazy, a bar and live music venue in the heart of the city centre. Sleazys, as it was affectionately known by Glaswegians, had been around since the early nineties, offering gig space in the basement along with good beer and a solid food menu. The tunes were always on point too.

Quinn had ordered some food while she waited for Lisa. She was eating one of Trusty Buck's plant-based burgers along with a large order of chips on the side. Not being much of a cook, this was one of those rare opportunities for her to get something substantial into her body. Today, Quinn was ravenous. She felt like she could eat two of those burgers and still have room. She was finishing up when she saw Lisa walking downstairs, making her way from the street into the bar, looking like someone who'd taken a wrong turn.

Quinn spun around on the barstool. She tossed the last few chips into her mouth, bobbing her head in time to 'Peaches' by The Stranglers.

"Hi," Lisa said, glancing around the bar. "It's empty in here, isn't it?"

"It's only just opened," Quinn said, mildly distracted by Lisa's appearance. How long since they'd last seen one another? Two days? Three. And yet Lisa's face was even more of a mask of sunken cheeks and hollow eyes than it had been last time. How long before every curve and edge of her skull was visible under the taut skin? It hadn't always been like that. Quinn had looked up Lisa's Facebook profile and even though the account was set to private there were still some old profile photos available for anyone to view. The woman in those photographs was a different person altogether. The old Lisa had been a much healthier weight. Big-boned. Strong. There'd been a sunny glow, a confidence in the eyes and a beaming smile.

"I didn't expect to hear from you so soon," Lisa said, her eyes still darting around the room. "Have you found something?"

Quinn nodded. She wiped the corners of her mouth with a napkin. Then she pushed the empty plate over the counter and mumbled her thanks to the barman who took it away. She slid off the barstool, feeling as full as she'd felt in a long time.

"I have. But before I get to that, is everything okay with you?"

Lisa shook her head. "I got another letter."

"Shit. When?"

"This morning."

"Bastards. What does it say?"

"Same thing as the last one," Lisa said, sounding hoarse and tired. "It's a reminder, although this one came with a specific time-sensitive warning. I've got forty-eight hours to do what I was ordered to do in the last letter."

"You mean, spread the love? Screw every homeless person in Glasgow?"

"Yes."

Lisa's eyes combed the surroundings yet again and Quinn realised that the poor woman was paranoid. She couldn't imagine how exhausting it must be living in Lisa's head. Always that feeling of being watched.

"Did the letter say anything else?" Quinn asked. "What happens if you don't do it?"

Lisa's narrow shoulders drooped. Her arms hung limp at the sides and Quinn had the impression of looking at a woman twice Lisa's age.

"Go public. That's been the threat from the start and I can't imagine it's changed. Whoever's doing this, they know what I'm afraid of. Of everyone finding out that I let my husband drown."

"They can't prove it," Quinn said. "It's their word against yours."

"One look at my face is all it'll take. I wouldn't last five minutes under interrogation."

"Lisa, maybe we should sit down. Get a table, aye? You look like you could do with taking the weight off your feet."

Lisa nodded. "I'm at the end of my rope here Quinn. And believe it or not, it's not just this letter. It's..."

"What?"

"I saw him again this morning. Tommy was at the bottom of the street, this wasn't long after I discovered the letter on the doorstep. He had his hands in his pockets and he was standing kind of stiff and upright the way he used to in public. I didn't go out. I knew he'd be gone by the time I got there.

Quinn shook her head. "Look, I don't doubt you saw someone. But it wasn't Tommy."

Lisa gazed at Quinn with a fixed, piercing stare. "Who then? Deb thinks someone is dressing up like Tommy and standing outside to torture me? Is that what you think too?"

"Honestly, I don't know."

"Then how do you know it's *not* Tommy?"

"I was clean when I came to your house," Quinn said. "There's nothing of his presence there, in the house, in the street. I'd have felt something that day. But there's nothing. Tommy's not there, except in your memory."

"If you say so."

"I do."

Lisa didn't look convinced. "So why am I here?"

Quinn smiled. "You want a drink first? You look like you could use one after a shitty morning."

Lisa made a face like she was about to throw up. "No thanks, I'm trying to cut it out of my life. Then again, look at you. You drink like it's a race and so far it doesn't seem to be doing you much harm. You're still functioning."

"I eat like a horse," Quinn said. "Whenever I can that is. You sure I can't order you a plate of something? The food's amazing here. It's a hundred percent plant-based menu and damn good eating, I swear. Do you good."

"No thanks."

"How about a juice? A Coke?"

"Water, thanks."

Quinn ordered the water. When they had their drinks, they relocated to a corner table near the stairs but not too close to any other occupied tables that their conversation might be overheard.

"Cheers," Quinn said, tapping the Peroni neck off Lisa's glass. She drank the beer, watching Lisa as discreetly as possible. She was still worried that Lisa was too frail. That she was about to pass out.

Lisa sipped the water, her long bony fingers wrapped tight around the glass. Then she looked at Quinn. "So what have you got for me?"

Quinn took a deep breath. She'd already decided to jump straight into the deep end. "There was a third person in the car when it crashed into the river."

Lisa's expression tightened. It was as if someone had pulled a cord on the woman's neck. "Are you serious?"

Quinn nodded. "I'm serious. Not only that, I'm pretty sure I know who it was."

"Who?"

"Did you see the window in the backseat?" Quinn asked. "When you were under? It's only visible in a handful of photos online. The one behind the driver's seat. It's rolled halfway down. More than halfway."

"I saw it," Lisa replied, "but I didn't take much notice at the time. It wasn't a significant gap, maybe a child could squeeze through it."

"Or someone very skinny."

"I suppose," Lisa said. "And who would that be?"

"Fran Buckley."

"Who's that?"

Quinn tried to contain the excitement in her voice. "She's Abbey's best friend. She's a fellow traveller, around twenty-years-old with a big chip on her shoulder. Pretty enough, but her default is resting bitch face. You might have seen her walking around your neighbourhood because she stayed in that student flat with Abbey, at least for a while. Turns out Abbey, for all her good looks and bravado, wasn't the most stable of human beings. Fran, well she's a lot tougher. She *was* in the car, I'm sure of it. Abbey kept her close like a kid clinging to a teddy bear. That's why Fran moved from the camp to the student flat. Inseparable, that's the word I heard. Plus she's as skinny as a rake. She could give you a run for your money."

"So what happened?" Lisa asked.

"I think Tommy called Abbey after you stormed out of the house that day. I think he called an early meeting with her before work. I think...I think he was going to break it off."

Lisa's eyes widened. She grabbed the water and took a frantic sip.

"Abbey sensed something was wrong," Quinn said. "So she brought Fran along for moral support. They meet in the car, all three of them."

"Why's Abbey driving?" Lisa asked.

"Maybe Tommy's trying to be nice. He feels bad. It's a pretty nifty car and Abbey's probably been after a shot for ages. So they're driving along. He lays it out, tells her it's over. Abbey freaks out and it's a big one. This girl is literally suicidal but I doubt Tommy knew about her previous attempts or he'd never have allowed her to drive. But now he regrets putting her behind the wheel. As for Fran, she regrets coming along for the ride. Abbey must have been so far gone she didn't think about her baby or her best friend in the backseat. She fantasised about dying underwater – that comes straight from Fran. It's Abbey's lucky day. There's a strip of wire fencing and it lets her get past the barrier. Boom. They're in the river. Fran panics. She squeezes through the back window, saves herself. Gets out of there before anyone sees her. Now she's wrestling with survivor's guilt every day."

Lisa blinked hard, processing the information.

"You didn't see anyone else?" Quinn asked. "In the water?"

Lisa closed her eyes. "It happened so fast. I suppose she could've gotten out through the window. Swam away unnoticed. But why would she leave her friend?"

"Survival instinct," Quinn said. "That's my guess. You said Abbey looked pretty dead, right?"

"Yeah, but she was unconscious. She drowned."

Quinn nodded. "My guess is that Fran panicked. What the hell, right? Most of us would if we found ourselves in a sinking car. It's only later on that the guilt and the 'what if' comes back to haunt us. Maybe she tells herself that Abbey was suicidal anyway. That it was her time."

"What about the letters?" Lisa asked.

Quinn took another sip of Peroni.

"I think Fran saw you. She saw you dive into the river from the footpath. Then she saw you go under and come back up empty-handed. No Tommy. No Abbey. Then, it gets interesting. You swam away without raising the alarm. You didn't scream yourself hoarse trying to draw attention to the river."

"I did call once," Lisa said. "Before I saw who was down there. Doesn't matter. Nobody heard me."

"Fran and Abbey were best friends," Quinn said. "Abbey knew your marriage to Tommy was in the pits and that means Fran knew. She's a sharp cookie. She put two and two together when you swam away quietly from the car like you did. Bingo. She's got you Lisa."

Lisa's brow furrowed. "Why did she wait a year to start harassing me?"

"Who knows?" Quinn said. "Those one-year anniversaries sting like a bitch. Besides, it would've taken some time for her to come to terms with not helping Abbey. But one year down the line, she was ready for you."

"This is too much," Lisa said, closing her eyes. "She *saw* me that day? Someone actually saw me climb out of the river?"

She took a sip of water. Sat in silence, blinking as if there was dust trapped in her eyes. "If Fran's doing this, why do I keep seeing Tommy?"

Quinn sighed. "Because he's in your head twenty-four seven. It's only natural that you might..."

"I'm not imagining it. I've seen Tommy at least three times now."

A pause.

"Why is this girl coming after me? She left Abbey to die. If what you're saying is correct then we both made the wrong choice."

"Fran hates you," Quinn said. "She hates everything you represent. You, the nice, middle-class woman that gets noticed. You've got a good job and society treats you well, aye? The media would label it a tragedy if you'd died in that car crash. Abbey? She was just another slutty traveller. She was completely passed over, allowing everyone to forget her. Now you've become the face of Fran's war against the world."

"Maybe I will have that drink," Lisa said, staring hungrily over at the bar.

"I'll get it."

Quinn pushed herself onto her feet. "Nothing you do will ever be enough for Fran. She's hurt, guilty, bitter and she's lashing out. She'll grind you down to dust, no matter what happens. Take my word for it."

"How do we stop this?" Lisa asked, her eyes wide and fearful.

Quinn started towards the bar. Then she paused, glanced over her shoulder. "Leave that to me. That's what you're paying me for."

20

Sixteen years to the day. That's how long it had been since Quinn's mother was murdered in that house.

The house Quinn was standing outside now.

Her body was like a clenched fist. Eyes locked on the old building. Her first home was a beautiful old Victorian house in Lenzie, an affluent area roughly eight miles northeast of the city centre. Two storeys. Amber ashlar, raised roof lantern on the main slate roof. Bay windows. Doric pilasters at the entrance. The old place hadn't changed much.

Nobody in Glasgow, besides a handful of exceptions, knew about Quinn's past. Most of them would pass out with shock if they knew she came from a well-off family in the leafy suburbs. They knew Quinn Hart, the punk rocker prone to strange headaches, scraping by on a month-to-month basis in a dump of a flat near the art school. Stubborn. Determined. Loyal. Hard-drinking. That's the person they knew. That's the person everyone knew.

But Quinn remembered someone else.

She stood across the street from the house. For appearances sake, she pretended to be on her phone, pressing her ear against the earpiece and nodding and mumbling gibberish every thirty seconds or so. There were people in the garden. A man, woman and two young boys in their early teens. All well-groomed, well-dressed, like most of the people who could afford to live on this exclusive street. The boys stood shoulder to shoulder, laughing at something on their phones. Their parents stood beside the car, a sleek Mercedes-Benz, in deep discussion.

Quinn stole a hurried drink from the hip flask in her side pocket. The flask was spilling over with Johnnie Walker but despite the whisky, the noise in Quinn's head was bubbling up like hot lava. It happened whenever she came back to Lenzie. Back to this house. And yet, Quinn could never resist the call.

A series of five random, seemingly unconnected murders within a two-year period had rocked the northeast region of Glasgow in the early 2000s. That series of killings ended here. The Lenzie murder or the Hart murder, as it was known at the time, was a sickening act committed by a man with no obvious motive. Survivor and eyewitness descriptions across all five murders tied the crimes together. A heavyset (or giant as one child had described him) man with a black balaclava over his head had broken into each house and killed the occupants in cold blood. Three murders took place in broad daylight while the remaining two occurred late at night. Nothing was ever stolen. There was no connection between the five sets of victims.

These were random killings. The press called him The Hammer. Not exactly an inspired choice, Quinn thought.

No children were ever killed in the attacks. Mostly it was women, although two men had also died over the course of the five incidents. Another thing the press had latched onto was that some of the kids, in the days leading up to the murders, had reported seeing a man in their bedroom late at night. He was standing over their bed. A heavyset man. A giant looking down at them.

Two kids gave the detectives a name.

Scooby.

Quinn hadn't seen anyone in her bedroom leading up to her mother's murder. All she recalled was the sight of her mother being bludgeoned to death in front of her. The sound of Beth Hart's voice during those last few moments of consciousness. Even at the end, she'd summoned a high-pitched scream telling Quinn to run. But Quinn didn't run. The killer butchered her mother, avoiding the black-haired girl's eyes. Then he left, covered in blood. Quinn was clutching her Etch A Sketch toy, pulling it close to her chest. It was the only thing left in between her and The Hammer.

Eyewitnesses said his breathing was loud. More like a wheeze, Quinn thought. She might even have said that to the police at the time but she couldn't remember what she'd said to all those ladies talking to her in a soft voice. Nice ladies, trying to prise snippets of valuable information out of her.

Quinn came back to the house to remember. To keep in touch with that quiet child, the one who'd loved art and books. Little Quinn, so sensitive and fragile. She never knew her father. He'd walked out on the family when Quinn was two but it didn't matter. He was a loser, her grandparents told her in later years. All talk and no trousers. The money came from Quinn's mother's side of the family and they coped perfectly well without her old man.

In the aftermath of the murder, after Quinn had been shipped off to her grandparents' house in Dollar, something frightening was happening to her. The noise. She told her grandparents about the violin-like screeching in her head but they, as well as the counsellors and everyone else, thought it was some kind of grief response. Trauma-induced. She heard that one a lot. Quinn stopped mentioning it after a while. No one understood. No one took her seriously and if she kept going on about it, she knew they'd lock her up in a madhouse.

She pulled the flask out of her pocket. Took something bigger than a sip.

What good was remembering?

The woman in the driveway had noticed Quinn. Quinn turned sideways, pressed the phone tighter to her ear and pretended she was talking to Lisa.

"I'm going to fix it. Trust me, I'm going to fix this mess, okay?"

How?

"Fran's smart but she doesn't know we're on to her. Next time she goes anywhere near your house, I'll be all over it."

How?

"I'm going to follow her."

Quinn inched back towards the house. The woman in the driveway was talking to her husband again.

What was she doing all this for? Was she ever going to admit to herself that there was a strong resemblance between Lisa Granger and Beth Hart? At least there would be if Lisa put a little more weight back on. She saw a woman in distress. A woman who looked like her mother and here was this fierce desire to crack the case.

Clarity. That's what the old house gave to Quinn. She could say things here, even if it was just to herself, that she couldn't say anywhere else. That's why she came back here. Every now and then, she needed a little reminder of who she was under the green hair and fuck you attitude.

She took her back off the wall. The couple in the

driveway were gawping at her again and Quinn could only imagine what she looked like to them. The green-haired girl in ripped jeans sipping from the hip flask, hanging out by herself across the street.

She set off towards the train station, wondering if the new owners had any inkling of what happened in that house.

With any luck, they didn't.

21

Quinn's green hair was buried under a beanie hat.

It wasn't a comfortable choice, seeing as how it was twenty-two degrees in the afternoon and Quinn hated the heat even when she wasn't overdressed. This *was* heat as far as Scotland was concerned. The sort of day when pale-skinned, vitamin D deprived northerners ripped off their shirts and strutted around topless, pink nipples sizzling in the sun.

Still, the hat was necessary. Quinn was tailing Fran Buckley.

It was busy in town. The traffic on Argyle Street, both human and vehicle, was a neverending parade of bodies and machines. It looked like the last Saturday before Christmas without the cold weather. But at least the bodies offered Quinn some cover. As long as she didn't lose Fran in the crowd, everything was good.

It had been a long day of surveillance so far. Quinn was up with the birds, shoving tea and toast down her throat before taking an Uber to the Stewarton Road site in Newton Mearns. After finding a secluded, grassy spot across from the traveller's car park, and making sure no one could see her, she'd settled down to watch. Unlike Quinn however, Fran wasn't an early riser. When the blond girl finally made an appearance outside one of the shabbier-looking caravans, Quinn had been sitting in the grass for over three hours. Fran looked the worse for wear. Hair like a bird's nest. Zombie walk. She wandered around the car park for a while, talking to some of the women, playing with the kids. Someone handed her a cup of something hot. Afterwards, Fran walked back into the caravan and closed the door.

Quinn watched and waited. She ate a Royal Gala apple, a family-sized bag of salt and vinegar crisps and after that she was chain-smoking cigarettes for Scotland. She hoped to God that Fran wasn't going to stay in all day. Quinn could just imagine Fran in that rundown caravan, sitting at the kitchen table with resting bitch face, typing out another 'Make It Up To Me' letter on an ancient typewriter with missing keys. Resting bitch face would morph into a twisted grin as she envisioned dropping it off on Lisa's doorstep.

"C'mon," Quinn said, sitting cross-legged on the grass. Her legs were starting to rebel against all this sitting.

Fran did go out eventually. She stepped out of the caravan, dressed in jeans and a green t-shirt with her blond hair tied back in a ponytail. She waved goodbye to those on the site and walked north. Quinn packed up and followed at a distance. When Fran signalled for a double decker bus on Kilmarnock Road, Quinn panicked. It was either run or lose Fran for the rest of the day. Quinn ran. She hated running. Not only did she run, she waved her arms like a madwoman, catching the driver's attention in the side mirror at the last second. She thanked him for stopping as she stepped on board and paid the fare. Quinn hurried down the aisle, keeping her head down. But Fran wasn't sitting on the lower deck. She was upstairs somewhere and with any luck, she hadn't noticed Quinn signalling the driver.

It was back on.

Quinn took a seat at the back of the bus. She leaned her shoulder against the window, still trying to catch her breath. Damn, she thought. Any more running and she'd have to consider joining a gym.

The bus travelled north onto Pollokshaws Road and made its way towards the busy city centre. Fran appeared beside the driver's cabin ahead of the upcoming Jamaica Street stop. Quinn's heavy eyelids were jolted open. She got up. Walked slowly down the aisle, hoping that Fran wouldn't turn around.

The bus stopped and the doors hissed open. Fran stepped off and Quinn followed, keeping her head down. Pulling the beanie lower over her forehead.

Fran took a left turn at the top of Jamaica Street where it merged onto Argyle Street. She walked in the direction of Central Station.

Quinn kept Fran in her line of vision at all times. Then she switched to the opposite side of the street to better avoid detection. She never took her eyes off the target, almost bumping into at least five people approaching from the bridge. None of them were happy with Quinn and they let her know all about it. Fuck this, Quinn thought. She was starting to loathe surveillance. It was boring and exhausting. It was late in the day and she was ready to murder a cold beer. Plus she was famished. All she'd eaten was some toast, an apple and some crisps. A full pack of Benson and Hedges was almost gone.

Her throat felt dry and tight. Like there was a hedgehog lodged in there.

Quinn's pursuit came to a stop as she watched Fran push

through the door of Tickets Scotland – a ticket agency located directly under the bridge.

"What are you doing now?" she asked.

Quinn lingered on the edge of the kerb, mindful of the busy traffic. Such a long day, she thought. Her legs were beat. Maybe instead of tailing Fran around the city in broad daylight, she thought, it would be more useful to find out what Fran was buying tickets for. Understand the girl's interests, that kind of thing. If she was going to a gig, Quinn could go too and keep an eye on her. Now that she had Lisa's money in her bank account, Quinn didn't need to worry about overspending. And it was for the investigation. Maybe she could start an expenses account.

Aye, she thought. Why not?

Fran exited the shop, tucking something deep into the back pocket of her pale jeans. Looked like she'd bought something.

She hesitated for a moment, then continued west along Argyle Street.

Quinn watched her go. She hoped she wouldn't regret the decision to stop tailing her. Hoped that no more letters would show up on Lisa's doorstep that day.

Quinn rushed across the street, narrowly avoiding a collision with a single-decker bus. The driver blared his horn and Quinn answered with the middle finger and a few colourful words before disappearing inside Tickets Scotland.

"Hi," she said, strolling up to the desk.

A tall man with a black Steven Seagal ponytail and a receding hairline at the temples stood behind the counter. He narrowed his eyes at Quinn's sudden approach. Looked like he'd been caught off-guard.

"Afternoon. Can I help you?"

"Did she buy three?" Quinn blurted out. She had her thumb jerked towards the door. Her heavy breathing, exaggerated so that Seagal would think she'd been running. "Three tickets? Is that right?"

Seagal pulled at the neck of his AC/DC vest top. Looked like he was trying to let some air into the skin. "Excuse me?"

"My friend. I'm just catching up with her on Argyle Street but I wanted to make sure she bought the right number of tickets. Talking about the wee skinny girl with the blonde hair who was just in here. She was literally just in your shop man. Green t-shirt. Wee Frannie Buckley. She bought three tickets, aye? Did she buy three tickets mate?"

Seagal knitted his brows. Then his eyes lit up as he put the pieces together. "For the Mogwai gig?"

"Aye, of course."

"She bought two."

"Two?"

"Two. She bought two tickets."

Quinn approached the counter, feigning a look of outrage. "You serious? For Mogwai at the..."

The pause was excruciating.

"Barrowlands," Seagal said. "Saturday night. Two tickets."

Mogwai. Barrowlands. Saturday night.

Quinn kept riffing off the top of her head. "I can't believe wee Frannie Buckley didn't shout me a ticket after all I've done for her. I don't know how many times that lassie's tapped me for a loan, know what I'm saying?"

Seagal glanced at his phone on the counter. "Aye. It's a scandal."

Quinn dug a hand into her pocket, fishing out her debit card. "Fine, whatever. I'll take one. I assume there's still tickets left?"

"A few, aye."

"Lucky me."

Quinn paid the man for a ticket to see Mogwai at the Barrowlands on the following night. She felt a sudden blast of exhilaration. Damn, she *was* pretty good at this PI stuff. Now she knew where Fran would be on Saturday night. At the Barrowlands, soaking up the tunes, getting drunk and then what next? Quinn had a fair idea of what would happen next. It would be off to Kelvindale in the dead of night to play midnight postwoman.

And Quinn would be there. Every step of the way.

Leaving Tickets Scotland, Quinn walked outside and crossed the road into Central Station. She took refuge in a quiet pub with a pint of Stella Artois.

As she drank, she thought about the Granger case. In particular, she was mulling over an emerging theory that had popped into her head during that morning's long surveillance in Newton Mearns.

Love triangle.

More precisely, a love triangle featuring Tommy Granger, Abbey Donaldson, and Fran Buckley. Tommy, the naughty boy who liked his woman young. Two for the price of one. Two bored traveller girls lusting after the bored husband with the fancy Audi. That would explain why Fran was in the car on the day of the crash if it wasn't just for moral support. What if she was getting dumped too?

Quinn noticed a sixty-something man, dressed in a Celtic top and blue jeans. He was sitting at the bar, not far from her table. He kept looking over at Quinn. Smiling. Waiting for the opportunity to pounce, Quinn thought. She knew he was going to make a move, forty-year age gap be damned.

She picked up her pint, then put it back down. No,

maybe a threesome was too far-fetched. Whether it was true or not, it didn't seem to have a bearing on what mattered most of all right now. The priority was catching Fran in the act of delivering those letters. Shine a torch in her eyes and let her look into the eyes of someone better. Someone smarter. Catching her was becoming an obsession for Quinn. She wanted to get that skinny bitch and get her bad.

Shit, she *was* obsessed.

There was one other question eating away at Quinn and it was one she couldn't seem to shake it off.

"Y'alright sweetheart? Mind if I..."

"Fuck off," Quinn snapped, growling at the grey-haired Casanova in the Celtic top who'd decided to make his move. He was coming over with two fresh whiskies in hand. The bite in Quinn's voice made the old-timer pirouette like a dancer and turn back to the bar.

"Slag," he whispered. Quinn heard it but she wasn't in the mood to throw a glass at his head.

Back to the question at hand, she thought.

Fran bought two tickets for the Mogwai gig. Two. Presumably, one for herself. But who was the second ticket for?

22

She was a silent and shadowy figure, standing across the street from the Barrowlands Ballroom. Tapping her index finger off the pointy tip of a guitar pick she'd pulled out of her pocket. Counting out the rhythm in her head, four beats to the bar.

It was Saturday night, a little after seven-thirty. Quinn had taken shelter from a light drizzle in the doorway of the Gallowgate flooring shop. She'd been there for an hour watching a steady convoy of gig-goers make their way towards the venue's front entrance. Heads were hidden under hoods or umbrellas or both. The rain was making it hard for Quinn to see their faces. To see the face she'd come to see.

There was still no sign of Fran. Since taking up position in the doorway, Quinn had been approached by two dirty old men asking if she was offering 'business'. A couple of others had shown interest too.

She lit up a cigarette. Even with Lisa's money propping up her bank account, Quinn couldn't afford to keep smoking like she was undertaking an experiment in a laboratory.

That was another problem with surveillance. All the waiting around. But what was she supposed to do if she couldn't smoke? Take up knitting?

Quinn glanced up towards a dense carpet of dark clouds. The sky felt like it was descending upon the city like a bad omen.

Patience, she told herself.

She stared across the street. The punters approached the Barrowlands from both sides, walking, getting out of Ubers and taxis and hurrying to join the queue that led to the door and two hulk-like bouncers. It was all very civilised. There was no rowdiness or drunken chancers trying to hustle their way in by pretending they were on the guest list. This was a Mogwai gig after all. Not exactly the sort of band you saw blind drunk or if you were looking for a fight. Sparse lyrics, sonic moods. That was Mogwai. A good stoner band but much more than that. The rowdies were most likely heading into the city centre pubs or nightclubs for something livelier.

Quinn pulled out her phone, dialled Lisa's number and leaned her shoulder against the doorway. She took a last drag of the cigarette and then stomped it to death on the top step.

"Hi Quinn."

"Lisa?"

"Yep, it's me."

Lisa sounded tired, Quinn thought. Hoarse and weak. She envisioned a haunted-looking skeleton on the other end of the line, two bony hands clutching a glass of wine.

"How you doing?"

"Okay," Lisa said. "You?"

"Never been better. You at home?"

"At a caring caller visit. Watching TV with Annette, the

woman I told you about. Hang on, I'm just going to step outside and take this. I'm talking over the film."

"Cool."

Quinn waited. She was still watching the door of the Barrowlands. When Lisa spoke again, her voice was louder and clearer.

"Sorry about that. It's easier to talk out here."

"No worries," Quinn said. "Caring caller, eh? Was that in the letters too?"

"Actually, I found this one by myself. I enjoy spending time with Annette. She's lovely and best of all, she knows nothing about all this other shit I'm going through. Yeah, she tells me to put weight on but that's it. Sometimes it feels like she's the one taking care of me rather than the other way around. I feel safe here. I don't feel like I'm being watched all the time."

"How's the drinking?"

"Tea. You?"

"It's different for me Lisa."

"I know."

Quinn watched as more people filed into the Barrowlands. Where the hell was Fran Buckley? And what if she didn't show up? What if she'd bought the tickets for someone else? A gift.

That would hurt.

"Where are you?" Lisa asked.

"Barrowlands. Waiting for you know who."

"Oh yeah, I forgot. Is she there yet?"

"Not yet, but there's still plenty of time. Did you get any more letters? Phone calls?"

"No," Lisa said. "But it's only a matter of time, isn't it? I haven't done what I've been told and I've ignored the reminder. Quinn, my nerves are shot to hell. They could make it public any minute now and then what's going to happen? I've got the police at the door? My mother-in-law and her family? All the newspapers?"

Quinn couldn't blame Lisa for fretting. "I'm on it. Try not to worry."

There was a deep sigh down the line.

"Thanks Quinn."

"Gotta go. Enjoy the telly and biscuits and old lady chat. I'll let you know if something happens."

"I'll try."

Quinn hung up and stepped onto the pavement. She was checking to see if it was still raining when Fran appeared across the street.

"Yes."

She felt a sudden adrenaline spike. All the boredom and frustration of the past hour were forgotten.

She walked to the kerb for a better view. Fran's skinny frame was insulated under a white hooded sweatshirt, denim jacket combo and a pair of dark blue tracksuit bottoms.

Her date walked beside her. A thick arm wrapped around her shoulders.

He was a big guy, almost twice Fran's height. He wore a long green parka with blue jeans and a black beanie to keep the rain off his head. Quinn had anticipated Fran turning up with Donnie as the other gig-goer. She didn't know this guy. Couldn't remember seeing him at the Newton Mearns camp during her visit to Donnie or during the long surveillance yesterday. Hadn't Fran said something about her boyfriend being a non-traveller? Her man was rock solid. Broad shoulders, thick arms. There was a swagger to his walk that suggested someone who didn't lack confidence.

The couple walked hand in hand, following the long

snake-like queue to the door. After a few words with the bouncer, they slipped inside with little fuss.

Quinn crossed the street, glad to leave the doorway behind and give it back to the sex workers. She joined the queue and when it was her turn to be assessed by the dour-faced bouncer duo, she smiled and looked them both in the eye. One of the Barrowlands' regular bouncers, a bearded hulk called James, barely gave Quinn a second glance.

"On you go hen."

"Cheers," Quinn said, hurrying inside before James recognised her. She recalled having a couple of run-ins with the big man in the past. Fortunately, her hair had been a different colour and length at the time.

The Barrowlands was slowly filling up. It was warm as Quinn made her way upstairs and her first stop was at the bar to grab a pint. She'd earned it after all that bullshit surveillance. She wriggled her way to the front of the small crowd, ordered a pint of Tennents and took it up to the spacious ballroom.

This was a spectacular venue, one loved by fans and musicians across the world. Quinn took a moment to reacquaint herself with a place that felt like an old friend. Wood-panelled walls, art deco lights and Avant-garde tiles. The arched ceiling with its sporadically-placed ceramic stars and diamonds. The best thing about the Barrowlands however, were the intangibles. It was the magic that stirred up inside the place whenever a band and crowd of Glaswegians got together for a good night. There were no bad gigs here.

Quinn leaned against one of the ballroom pillars. She drank her beer, peering over the plastic rim of the cup in search of Fran and her date. The venue wasn't full yet. The lights were still up. A moment later, she spotted the couple standing close to the stage. They were dancing to the warm up tunes. Both had a beer in hand and both were gazing adoringly into the eyes of the other. Nothing else seemed to exist, only the music and the person in front of them.

Quinn watched from a safe distance. She nursed her beer, brushing off a couple of sweaty-faced guys that offered to buy her a drink. Shining knights who wanted to save her from being alone.

About ten minutes later, Donnie showed up. Dancing. Hugging everyone as if they were long lost siblings. Even from afar, Quinn could tell that Donnie's eyes were like two flying saucers. The big man was on pills and God knows what else. He embraced Fran, almost falling on top of her. He shook hands with Fran's date before pulling him in for a bear hug. For the next ten minutes, Donnie, along with Fran and her boyfriend, danced to the electro pop pumping out of the speakers.

Quinn watched and waited. An opportunity finally arose when Fran handed her beer cup to her boyfriend. She pulled her man down, kissed him hard on the lips and then whispered something in his ear.

Then she walked towards the women's bathroom.

"Fuck it," Quinn said.

She placed her beer cup on the floor and followed Fran to the bathroom. With a deep breath, she pushed the door to the ladies' room open. Walked inside.

Two of the cubicle doors were closed. Quinn, not entirely sure of what she was doing, walked over to the sink. She ran the hot water tap, washed her hands and then grabbed a paper towel to dry them. She saw her reflection in the mirror. Saw a flicker of apprehension in those blue eyes. Quinn gave a nod of encouragement to herself, then concentrated on the cubicle doors behind her.

She heard a flush. A lock snapped open. Quinn

continued to dry her hands as Fran stepped out of the cubicle.

What if she doesn't remember you?

Quinn scrubbed her hands raw with the paper towel. When she glanced in the mirror, Fran was standing in the cubicle doorway. She was staring at Quinn.

"I know you," she said in that deep voice so at odds with the waif-like appearance. "Lassie with the green hair. Quinn, aye? You came down to the camp and gave Donnie a fake number, eh? He was raging by the way. You never even bought any gear."

Quinn smiled. "Donnie was fast asleep when I left."

"Still," Fran said. "You got a few free smokes while you were in his caravan. Aye?"

"Guess so. No harm done, eh? Not like I stole anything on the way out although it wouldn't have been hard."

Fran walked over to the sink, hesitated for a second as if the taps might be boobytrapped. Then she washed her hands, still looking at Quinn in the mirror.

"You a Mogwai fan?"

"Sometimes," Quinn said, still scraping that shrivelled paper towel over what was left of her hands.

"Favourite album?"

Quinn didn't hesitate. "*Happy Songs for Happy People*."

Fran looked disappointed. "Oh aye."

"Thought I saw you at the door earlier," Quinn said. "Was that you coming in with the big guy in the green parka? That your mate? Boyfriend?"

Fran turned the hot water off. "Both."

Quinn grabbed another paper towel from the dispenser. "Finally moved on then?"

"Eh?"

"I said, you've finally moved on from Tommy Granger."

Fran scowled, her lip curling in disgust. "Tommy Granger? What the fuck are you talking about?"

"Nothing," Quinn said, shaking her head. "It's just that Donnie gave me the impression that you, Abbey and Tommy were all...well, you know?"

"All what?"

"Together."

Fran spat out a vicious laugh. "Donnie's a fat cunt who knows fuck all except how to deal drugs."

"I wouldn't blame you if it was true," Quinn said, turning towards Fran. She winked. "Good-looking guy like Tommy. Flash car. Bit of money in the bank. Why not share him with your best mate?"

The look of disgust was still evident on Fran's face. "You don't know anything, alright? I suggest you piss off and mind your own business."

With that, Fran barged past Quinn on her way towards the door. It was a brief collision of shoulders and Quinn felt the woman's collarbone jutting out. It was as good as a sharp blade attached to her body.

"Nothing wrong with a threesome," Quinn said, calling after Fran. "Bit of harmless fun, eh? Thing is Fran, I just wanted to put it out there."

Fran paused at the door. "Put it out there?"

"Aye. Listen, you don't have to give me an answer now. But if you and your man are interested...tonight, I mean. It's available, let's put it that way."

She smiled.

Fran's eyes narrowed, confused and suspicious. With a soft grunt, she stormed out of the bathroom and Quinn cursed herself for rushing in. Fran Buckley was a closed book. It felt like it would take years to get to know someone like that. Still, Quinn thought, she'd made a few cracks on the surface. She just hoped she hadn't blown it.

Quinn dropped the paper towel in the bin and returned to the venue with hands that had never been cleaner. She squeezed through the growing crowd. Found the remains of her pint on the floor. Decided against finishing it. Anyone could have dropped something into the cup during her absence. This was a work night and Quinn had no intention of falling into any date rape diversion trap.

She felt a tap on the shoulder. When she turned around, Fran was standing right in front of her. To Quinn's surprise, there was a smile on the girl's face. A display of friendliness that made her look like a different person to the one who'd stormed out of the bathroom a few minutes earlier.

"Sorry if I snapped back there," Fran said, leaning into Quinn's ear to make herself heard over the warm-up music.

Quinn shrugged. "It's cool."

"It's just," Fran said, the smile dissolving, "anything about Abbey gets me going. You know? I'm still trying to get over what happened."

Quinn felt Fran's fingers run down the side of her arm. She flinched at this unexpected contact, hoped Fran didn't notice.

"I get it."

"No hard feelings, eh?" Fran said, backing off.

"Nah."

"Enjoy the gig Quinn."

"Cool. You too."

Fran started to walk away, then she stopped and turned back to Quinn. "Oh and by the way..."

"Aye?"

"You were right. Three *is* the magic number. Maybe we'll

see you after the gig, my man and me. If you're still up for it?"

Quinn nodded. Tried to summon up a look of excitement but all she could manage was a wave of the hand. She leaned against the pillar, watching Fran as she walked back over to where her boyfriend was waiting by the stage.

Mogwai came onstage fifteen minutes later. The crowd cheered and the lights in the Barrowlands dimmed. Fran and her boyfriend, whilst watching the gig, also seemed to be moving away from the stage and getting closer to Quinn. Every now and then, she'd catch one of them staring in her direction whenever the lights were up. Donnie was gone, nowhere to be see. Quinn figured he'd probably passed out in the toilet.

Shit, she thought, watching the couple creep closer to her. Lisa, you're not paying me enough.

This strange back and forth between Quinn, Fran and her boyfriend lasted throughout the entirety of the gig. Quinn decided to go with it. This was one way of getting close to Fran and finding out more about the girl's vendetta against Lisa. Screw it. She danced flirtatiously, reeling them in further. Now she was going for it. The gig ended and the lights came up in the ballroom. The three of them got talking. Fran was tipsy by now, still friendly towards Quinn and far removed from the sulky, crusading girl that Quinn had first met in Donnie's caravan. The boyfriend was quiet. Intense. Not a bad-looking guy but blatantly undressing Quinn with his eyes. Fran must have seen it too, but she didn't seem to have a problem with it.

There was little doubt where all this was heading. Was Quinn really that committed to the job that she was willing to go to bed with these people? Both of them? She wasn't remotely drunk enough for this shit. And what would Lisa say if she found out? What would anyone say?

The Barrowlands emptied quickly. After two hours of live music, the floor was a sticky carpet of spilled beer and discarded plastic cups.

"Up for a party then?" Fran asked, brushing her arm up against Quinn's shoulder. The girl's skin was hot and smooth. She bumped into Quinn several times after that. All Quinn could feel was that same sensation of hard bone pressing into her. Fran's body was as meatless as a Linda McCartney burger.

"Always," Quinn said. "What do you have in mind?"

"I've got a flat near here," the boyfriend said. His voice was gruff. Like Fran, he possessed the voice of someone much older than the face suggested. He leaned his head into Quinn's face, his breath a rancid cocktail of stale beer and cigarettes. "Got some beers in the fridge. Some of Donnie's weed. Me and Fran are heading back now. Coming?"

Quinn glanced towards the stage. The roadies were already stripping down the band's backline. "Where's Donnie?"

"God knows," Fran said. "Probably dealing outside and making a fortune. Why? Do you really want Donnie to come to the party?"

"No chance."

"My van's parked just down the road," the boyfriend said. Quinn sensed a hint of impatience creeping into his voice, even if he was maintaining that grimace-like grin. "We'll be there in ten minutes if we go now. You up for a party, aye?"

"Parrrrrrtttty," Fran said, giggling as she finished the last of her beer. She threw the empty cup onto the floor. "Fuck it man, the night's young."

Quinn allowed a smile to creep onto her face. "Cool. Let's go."

The trio dragged their feet over the sticky floor. They hurried downstairs, exiting the Barrowlands with the last of the stragglers. The rain had stopped outside. The air was mild and the city sounded alive with people.

At the door, they took a left down the Gallowgate.

"That's me over there," the boyfriend said after a short walk. He was pointing at a dirty white transit van parked outside the African and Caribbean supermarket. "It's only a two-seater though. You cool to sit in the back till we get there?"

"The back?" Quinn asked.

"Aye, it's only a five-minute drive."

That's when Quinn heard the alarm bells ringing in her head. Loud and clear. All of a sudden, this undercover thing didn't seem like such a good idea. What the fuck had she done? And was there any way out before it was too late?

"Aye," she mumbled. "I suppose."

The boyfriend pulled open the back doors. Quinn found herself staring into the back of the van – a black hole that reeked of rotten fish.

"Stinks man," she said, recoiling at the foul odour. "What the fuck's been in there?"

Another gruff response.

"C'mon. In you go."

Quinn backed away from the door. She was on her tiptoes, trying to be silent. "I can't handle the reek in there man. That's vile. How about you give me the address? I'll get an Uber and..."

The boyfriend pushed her back towards the open doors. He charged forward. Swung his giant fist at Quinn. It was a vicious, clubbing blow that landed clean, rattling all the circuits in her head. Her body slammed into one of the van doors. The taste of blood in her mouth came fast. A second blow, just as hard, landed from behind. Quinn felt her feet leave the ground and then a dizzying, rollercoaster motion as she was hoisted into the back of the van. She rolled around on the hard, metallic floor, drowning in that horrible smell.

Fran's voice was a sharp, cutting hiss from behind. "Not as smart as you think you are, eh? Fucking bitch."

Quinn heard a deafening thud as the boyfriend jumped in the back. His feet on the van floor sounded like two giant hammers hitting metal. He rolled up his sleeves, hit her again and didn't stop till she was out cold.

PART 3 - CITY OF THE DEAD

23

LISA

Lisa's Toyota Corolla was parked in the driveway. It was deathly silent inside the car and her hands still gripped the wheel.

She was looking at the house. At the windows. At the doorstep.

She'd just arrived back from Annette's house. The two women had spent a pleasant Saturday night in front of the TV, drinking tea, eating biscuits and sandwiches, and talking. Lisa hadn't wanted to leave. She felt safe in Annette's flat, surrounded by familiar landscape paintings and framed photographs of people who didn't know her. She'd only left because Annette was dozing in her chair and Lisa realised, long overdue, that she was keeping the poor woman out her bed. After helping Annette get ready for bed, she hurried out to her car which was parked directly in front of the ground-floor flat.

Now she was back. Home. It was a little after ten o'clock and there were no lights on in the house. Lisa had forgotten to switch them on. What was the point? The lights wouldn't make the place look any more inviting.

At least there was nothing waiting for her on the doorstep. No final demands from her tormentor.

Her phone pinged on the passenger seat. Lisa, grateful for the distraction, fished it out of her bag and saw a text from Quinn Hart.

Got big news to share. We need to meet somewhere quiet and ASAP. Hurry, I'm being watched. Meet me at Necropolis. Come now.

Lisa's nose wrinkled up. She read the message a second time. The Necropolis? Why on earth did Quinn want to meet in a creepy old cemetery of all places and at this time of night?

Hurry, I'm being watched.

Lisa sighed. She glanced at her ghost-like reflection in the rearview mirror. If nothing else, a late-night trip to the Necropolis was a reason to avoid going into the dark, empty house in front of her. Fine, she thought. She dropped the phone in her bag and fired up the engine. Then she backed the Corolla out the driveway, turning the back so fast that the tyres made a light shrieking noise on the road. Elsewhere, the street was quiet. All the blinds and curtains were pulled shut. Lisa envied the safety that emanated from every other house. Yes, she'd done a terrible thing one year ago. But would the punishment ever end? After all, he'd betrayed her first, hadn't he?

Before driving off, Lisa realised she hadn't replied to Quinn. She took her phone out the bag and typed out a succinct reply.

On my way.

24

QUINN

It was another beautiful morning in Lenzie and six-year-old Quinn Hart was sitting cross-legged in the living room.

That morning, the chaffinches had been singing their short, rattling song in the garden. Quinn hoped the birds were blessing the house but her gran had once told her that singing birds meant the rain was coming. Rain didn't bother Quinn, a shy child, happy indoors and never lonely as long as she had her imagination to keep her company. Today, as she sat on the living room rug, she was playing with the anniversary edition Etch a Sketch that her mother had given her. Beth Hart had always encouraged her daughter's artistic side, urging her to write and draw, providing her with fresh notepads, crayons, felt tips and whatever else she needed. Sometimes Quinn drew her dad. There were no photographs of her dad in the house so Quinn used her imagination to fill in the giant blank that was her old man. She gave him a head that was too big for his body. Black hair. Square feet. One arm was always longer than the other.

He was imperfect. Her mother told her it was a good likeness.

Quinn was drawing a family of giraffes when she heard the first thud. There was little time to think about it. The second thud came and it sounded like a cannon going off outside the house. Quinn wasn't afraid at first, just confused and startled. Sometimes men would dig up the road outside and it would be noisy for hours. The fear came when she looked at her mum and saw her standing on her feet in a rigid, upright stance. The expression on Beth's face made her look like someone else. She had her fists clenched at her sides. Eyes bulging with fear as she stared through the living room doorway, down the hall and towards the front door. Up until that moment, Quinn had always believed that her mum wasn't scared of anything.

Beth whispered a word. "Run."

Quinn sat there, confused. Had there been an accident? Had someone driven a car into the front of the house?

Another thud, followed by a loud crashing noise.

It sounded like a stampede of wildebeest running around the house. Beth looked at Quinn, saying that word over and over again. "Run." Her mother leapt in front of the door, arms outstretched as if turning herself into a human wall. Then Quinn saw him. The man in the balaclava. He stormed through the open doorway, the sledgehammer cocked over his shoulder. It was the first and last time Quinn heard her mother scream. Beth ran towards him. He cracked her on the skull and the house shivered under Quinn. Beth toppled to the floor. She told Quinn to run again but it was hard for her to speak and the word was lost in her dying gasps. Quinn recalled the sound of her mum's skull being split open. A giant eggshell cracking open. The man didn't stop hitting Beth with the sledgehammer, even after she'd stopped moving. A pool of dark blood had gathered around her mother's head. It was flowing across the floor, creeping towards Quinn and her toys.

She woke up, gasping for air.

There was a throbbing pain around Quinn's temple and it felt like someone sawing her skull in half. As her senses rebooted, she tried to take in her surroundings. It was dark. She was sitting upright, her back pressed up against...

She turned around.

...a towering Celtic Cross headstone that had to be least eight feet tall.

Quinn blinked hard. Her eyes slowly adjusted and she saw headstones everywhere.

Barrowlands. Fran Buckley. The boyfriend. The fishy smell in the van and...

"Oh fuck."

She saw the outline of a tall spire in the distance. Behind that, the glittering city lights seemed to stretch on for miles. She thought about the headstones. The spire. Was she in Glasgow Cathedral? Not the cathedral itself, but the big sprawling cemetery in its shadow. The one that had fascinated Quinn during a brief goth phase in her late teens. The Necropolis. Glasgow's city of the dead.

A beam of torchlight pecked at Quinn's eyes. She winced, batting the light away with her hand.

"She's awake."

A woman's voice. Fran's voice.

"What the fuck's going on?" Quinn asked, her voice as limp and groggy as she felt. Talking made her head hurt even more.

There was no answer. Quinn sat up further, double-checking her surroundings.

It *had* to be the Necropolis.

The Victorian era cemetery, inspired by the world famous Père Lachaise Cemetery in Paris, was built on a rocky hill adjacent to Glasgow Cathedral. Thirty-seven acres, home to fifty-five thousand bodies although only a few thousand of those had monuments. Nowadays, the Necropolis stood as an outdoor museum to the work of the leading Scottish architects of the day. After dark, it became something else. It took a brave soul to wander alone there at night, such were the stories of hauntings and vampires.

Quinn was sitting on an isolated strip of damp grass by the footpath. The landscape around her was hilly and heavily vegetated. There was a grassy slope directly across the footpath, leading down to more tombstones and a cluster of gnarly-limbed trees that stood watch over the dead.

Footsteps scraped over the concrete path. Fran appeared, stopping a short distance ahead of Quinn. The torchlight flickered in her hands. She was still dressed the same as she'd been in the Barrowlands.

"I asked you a question," Quinn said. "What the fuck is going on? Why did you bring me here?"

Fran put the torch against her chin, shining the light upwards onto her face. She looked like she was about to tell creepy campfire stories.

"Like I said. Not quite as smart as you think you are, eh?"

"What are you talking about?"

"Let me tell you a wee story," Fran said, pulling the hood of the sweater over her head. Her features dissolved into darkness while her long blonde hair spilled out at both sides. "Once upon a time, I'm sitting in my caravan chilling with my man and listening to tunes. I hear a strange voice outside in the car park. So I look through the window and see this green-haired lassie on the site. I get up. I go out. I ask around. Margaret tells me you're looking for Donnie. You hear that? I was watching when you arrived. I didn't show up at Donnie's caravan to smoke weed. I knew there was something off about you the moment I laid eyes on you. So I walk into Donnie's caravan, sit down and all you want to do is talk about Abbey."

Quinn groaned. So much for being good at the job. And so much for subtle.

Fran's boyfriend appeared, standing at the crest of the slope.

"Surprised you woke up," he grunted.

Quinn had flashbacks to the savage beating she'd taken in the back of the van. All things considered, she'd come out of it okay. Her head hurt. There'd be bumps and bruises in the morning but it was doubtful she'd be alive to see them.

"I've been hit worse. By girls."

The boyfriend glared at her.

"I saw you following me yesterday," Fran said, still taunting Quinn. "Think I didn't see you running for that bus on Kilmarnock Road? Or buying tickets for Mogwai? And you thought you were watching me, eh?"

Quinn felt her confidence gushing out like water from a broken tap. If she was a PI, she was the worst PI that had ever lived. Didn't look like she was going to get the opportunity to improve either.

"Know where else I saw you?" Fran asked.

"In your dreams?"

"I saw you with Lisa Granger in Sleazys. Looked like you were having a right good natter about something."

Of course you did, Quinn thought. Because you were

following me as soon as I left Donnie's caravan. You followed me to the river. To Sleazys. And there was me thinking it was the other way around.

Fran and her boyfriend were two dark silhouettes framed in a bubble of torchlight.

"What did that Granger bitch hire you for?" Fran asked. "What exactly does she want to know?"

Quinn's answer was the middle finger. It was stupid and juvenile and yet she couldn't help herself. The boyfriend charged across the path like a bull to a red rag. He hoisted his leg in the air and came down hard with the flat of his boot on Quinn's chest. She went down onto her back. Felt the wind knocked out of her.

"Talk!"

He grabbed her by the collar, dragged her up to her feet as if she weighed no more than a ragdoll. Quinn's legs weren't all there. Two pillars of jelly, that's all she had underneath her right now. The boyfriend shoved her and she spun around, falling hard and landing on her stomach. Her head missed the granite cross by inches.

The boyfriend towered over her, cocking back a fist. His lip curled into a snarl. "What's she paying you for?"

"What do you think she's paying me for?" Quinn said, rolling over in the dirt. She was on her back, pushing it up against the cross for support. God, was there any part of her that didn't hurt? She spat dirt out of her mouth. "She wants to know why her dead husband is sending her those fucked up letters."

Quinn managed a smile. It hurt her battered jaw but it was worth it to see the confusion on their faces.

"I already know," she said. "Figured it out a while back actually."

Fran's eyebrows formed a stiff arch.

"You know what?"

"I know you were in the car when it hit the water," Quinn said. She pushed herself back to her feet, wiping the dirt off her hands.

Fran threw a worried glance at her boyfriend. Then she looked back at Quinn. "You don't know shit."

Quinn's hand swooped downwards. She made a splashing noise with her mouth.

"Car goes into the water. It floats for a while and at that point most people try to get the hell out. But Abbey's unconscious after hitting her head off the wheel, right? Airbags didn't deploy for some reason. She wasn't wearing her seatbelt. Meanwhile, Tommy's panicking in the passenger seat. He tries to help her but he knows he's running out of time. The engine weighs the front half of the car down. It starts sinking quick."

Fran's hateful expression thawed. "I heard the crunch when Abbey's head hit the steering wheel. She was dead, even if they say she drowned. No one could survive that."

"So you *were* there?" Quinn asked.

The torchlight trembled.

"You heard a crunching noise," Quinn said. "But how do you know Abbey was dead?"

"She was dead."

Quinn nodded. "I get it. Was that something you told yourself later? After you made the decision to abandon her? After you squeezed through the gap in the window and swam to safety?"

"You don't know what you're talking about," Fran said.

"I'm not judging you Fran. I'm sure it's a terrifying experience. The water rushes in through the windows, through the door frames. The electrics work for how long after you hit the water? Sixty seconds? That's not a lot of time to think straight. Friendship? Loyalty? Decency? Fuck that, right?"

Quinn caught her breath. Her headache was splitting and talking made it worse.

Fran aimed the beam of light at Quinn's face. "I thought you said you knew what happened."

"I know you bailed on Abbey. I know you like the wind on your face when you're in a car so you had the window open and when you guys landed in the river, you saw a way out for yourself. It was right there beside you. You made the decision to abandon your pregnant friend. To let her die. And then you had to live with it."

"It's a great story," Fran said. "But you're not giving me enough credit."

Quinn leaned back against the cross. Her eyes darted back and forth between Fran and the boyfriend. "What do you mean?"

Fran was silent.

"Alright then," Quinn said. "Tell me this much at least – what the hell were the three of you doing in Clydebank? Tommy was breaking it off with Abbey, I get it. But why go there?"

Fran sighed. She tapped her fingers off her belly three times.

"Clinic."

Quinn leapt off the headstone. She tilted her head in confusion. "What?"

"You heard," the boyfriend said.

"Clinic. As in...?"

Fran nodded.

"Oh shit," Quinn said. She felt like she'd been kicked in the face. "You were in Clydebank because there's a clinic there. Because Abbey was scheduled to have an abortion."

"There you go," Fran said, giving Quinn a round of stilted applause. "Now you're actually getting somewhere."

Quinn felt the jigsaw pieces rearranging themselves in her head. Not for the first time. But there were still more questions than answers. "Okay. Why was Abbey driving the car? Was it because Tommy wanted to distract her from the...*procedure*?"

"She was terrified," Fran said, talking through clenched teeth. "She'd always liked cars as long as I can remember. Her dad's a mechanic and she used to help him fix old bangers up. She liked that flash Audi. Said as much as soon as she saw it. It was Tommy's idea to let her drive from the flat to Clydebank. If she was concentrating on the road, he figured, she wouldn't be thinking about the abortion. Obsessing about it. He was being nice to her. On the way, he tried to remind her about the career she was going to have as a primary school teacher. How a kid would interfere with her studies. He kept saying she was doing the right thing."

"Abbey had a licence?"

"Nope. But she knew how to drive. She was a bloody good driver too."

"Didn't work though," Quinn said. "Did it? Driving Tommy's car didn't take her mind off what was about to happen."

Fran cleared her throat. Stole a quick glance at her boyfriend. "We were almost there. We almost made it. But Abbey's brain wasn't wired to handle that kind of shit. She was too fragile and when she freaked out, it wasn't just a regular freak out. It was big time."

"Let me guess," Quinn said. "Abbey didn't want to get rid of the kid? It was Daddy's decision."

"Bingo."

Quinn nodded. "That was another reason why Tommy was being so nice to her, eh? The prick felt guilty."

Fran and the boyfriend exchanged a subtle glance. There was a long, cutting silence inside the Necropolis.

"Tommy wasn't the father," Fran said. "He had nothing to do with Abbey getting knocked up."

Quinn felt a cold sensation in the pit of her stomach.

"What?"

The boyfriend stared at Quinn. There was a tight-lipped smile on his face. He gave a casual shrug of the shoulders, then pulled the beanie off his head to reveal a tousled mop of curly blond hair. "Ta-da."

Quinn felt like a giant, gaping hole had opened up underneath her feet. Tommy Granger was standing in front of her. No, that was impossible. Tommy Granger was dead. This was a younger version. Identical in almost every way – same face, same hair, same build.

"Who the hell are you?"

The boyfriend smirked. Revelling in Quinn's confusion.

"Tommy's nephew," Fran said, breaking the silence.

"Nephew?" Quinn said, her head spinning. "Holy shit. You're the one Lisa saw standing outside the hotel in Edinburgh. You're the 'Tommy' she saw on the street. His nephew? She told me about you once. Said you and the old granny in the wheelchair were the only decent ones in Tommy's family. Ewan – that's your name, right?"

"See now?" Fran said. "How far off the mark you were. Not much of an investigator, are you?"

Quinn stabbed a finger in Ewan's direction. "It was *your* baby?"

"Tommy was doing us a favour," Fran said. "He stepped up. Ewan's mum and gran would have flipped their lid if they found out that Ewan got a lassie pregnant. There was no way we were telling Abbey's dad either. Tommy was the only one Ewan trusted to help us. And he did. He booked the appointment. Scheduled it first thing in the morning because knowing what Abbey was like, we didn't want it hanging over her head all day. He offered to drive Abbey to the clinic. We would show up super early. Get her prepared. Tommy was a good guy. He was only trying to help."

Quinn thought about Lisa. About what she did in the river. About why she'd done it and what she'd gone through over the past year because of it. How would Lisa cope with the news that Tommy hadn't been cheating on her?

"Abbey wanted the baby," Quinn said. She was looking at Ewan. "She wanted it more than anything but you didn't. You didn't even have the balls to go to the clinic with her. Or maybe you just didn't care enough."

She pointed at the couple on the path. In the dark, they resembled a two-headed monster.

"And now you two are together?"

Quinn nodded. "You were together *before* Abbey died. And let me guess – Abbey's earlier suicide attempts. She was distraught because she suspected her boyfriend was cheating on her. Right?"

Quinn saw the flicker of discomfort in their eyes. Up until now, they'd been untouchable but she'd touched a nerve. She was getting to them and yet Quinn sensed there was something more. Something else that even now, with Quinn at their mercy in the Necropolis, they wanted to keep hidden.

And then it hit her.

"You wanted Abbey out of the way," she said to Fran. "She was the only thing standing in between you two fuck-heads getting together. Her and the baby. When she freaked out behind the wheel, what did you do Fran? Did you try to calm her down? Or did you encourage her?"

Fran shook her head. There was enough torchlight for Quinn to register the quiet horror etched deep on her face. "I tried to help her."

"Abbey freaked out," Ewan said. "She drove the car into the river."

Quinn nodded. "I don't doubt that Abbey freaked out. And when she did, I'm willing to bet that Fran dialled that panic button up even further."

Fran shook her head again. "No."

"Game's up Frannie. It's written all over your face. Nobody in the world knew Abbey better than you did. You knew she wasn't going to make it to that clinic without a full-on nervous breakdown. I'll bet you were filling her head with scary shit the night before too. Winding her up when you should have been protecting her. It wasn't Tommy's idea to let her drive, was it? I can picture it. Abbey freaks out behind the wheel. Instead of helping Tommy to calm her down, you start piling it on, taking advantage of her suicidal state of mind. You're screaming at her. Telling her it's hopeless. Telling her that Ewan doesn't love her. You drove her crazy. Told her it was better to die."

Ewan glanced at Fran. "Smarter than she looks."

"I'm good at joining the dots," Quinn said. "I might have been slow this time. But I got there in the end."

Fran looked close to tears.

"What happened?" Quinn asked.

"Tommy was yelling at me to shut up. He was telling Abbey not to listen to me. But I was Abbey's best friend and she loved me. I knew she was listening to me. I told her to look at the river – to concentrate on nothing except the river.

Tommy didn't think she'd do it. He thought he'd be able to talk her down. We were fighting for her soul."

"But you knew better Fran," Quinn said. "You knew there was no way the car would go into the river because of the steel barrier. That's why, as Abbey raced the car downhill towards the water, you leaned forward and unbuckled her seatbelt. Because there's no way Tommy would have let a pregnant woman drive without fastening her seatbelt first."

Fran wiped a tear off her cheek.

"Best friends?" Quinn said, shaking her head. "Who needs enemies, right?"

"Abbey was doomed," Fran said. "A girl like that, with all those hang-ups, she wasn't long for this world."

"What about Tommy?" Quinn asked. "You said it yourself – he was a good guy. He was only trying to help. And you were prepared to take him out too?"

"Tommy had his seatbelt on," Fran said. "He was only supposed to walk away with cuts and bruises. So was I."

Quinn thought back to what Lisa had told her about the events of that morning. About the car swerving erratically before it hit the water. Had Tommy, realising too late that Abbey was serious, tried to pull her off the wheel?

"You didn't know the barrier was undergoing repairs, did you?" Quinn said to Fran. "Didn't know about that temporary strip of wire fencing."

"That was a surprise," Fran said.

Quinn turned to Ewan. Her body was trembling with anger. "What the fuck is wrong with you? She killed your uncle and you love her for it? Are you insane?"

Ewan's eye twitched at the corner. "Uncle Tommy wasn't supposed to die."

"Except he did," Quinn said. "The car went through the

fence, hit the water and he stayed inside to help Abbey. Meanwhile, slippery Fran's out the window. Plan A turned to Plan B but you still got the result you wanted. Abbey and the baby are dead. And you guys are free to get it on in public."

Fran's voice dripped with contempt. "What about Lisa Granger? Do you judge her too? She left Tommy. She's no better than I am."

Quinn couldn't believe what was she was hearing.

"Lisa thought Tommy was cheating on her. Again! Yes, she fucked up but it's nothing compared to what you did. You killed your best friend. Why the hell are you writing those stupid letters to Lisa? Making out that Tommy's back from the dead. The fuck is wrong with you?"

Fran stabbed the torchlight in Quinn's eyes. "Because that rich bitch got all the sympathy in the papers. Abbey was ignored. They fucking ignored her!"

"You killed her," Quinn said. "What the fuck do you care about Abbey? You killed her."

"She was still a traveller. Still one of us."

Quinn nodded. "So you lay low for a year, waiting for the heat to die down. Then you turn it into a crusade. Travellers against the world. And Lisa Granger is the world."

She pointed at Ewan.

"You and Tommy were tight. Best buds, Lisa told me. That's how you knew Lisa's nickname. That's how you knew about the Menorca thing too. Tommy let you in on these little things. Right? Probably seemed harmless and yet it turned out to be great ammo to use against Lisa."

Ewan shrugged. "Enough talking. It's late and we need to be ready. We've got a guest coming."

Quinn looked at them both. "A guest?"

"Aye," Ewan said. "Auntie Lisa's on her way as we speak."

Quinn felt an icy coldness running down her spine. "Lisa? Why would she come here at this time of night?"

"Because you sent her a text," Ewan said, digging a hand into his pocket and pulling out Quinn's iPhone.

Quinn felt like throwing up.

"We used your finger to unlock it while you were out cold," Ewan said in his gruff voice. "Technology's amazing, eh? Then we arranged a meeting. Apparently, you've got big news to share."

25

LISA

It was a fifteen-minute drive from Lisa's house to the Necropolis.

Twice on the way, she caught herself going over eighty. Each time, Lisa hit the brakes, bringing the car down to a respectable fifty miles per hour. She was convinced that a swarm of sirens and flashing lights would be all over her in seconds. It didn't happen. She had to keep it together although her anxiety levels were shooting through the roof.

She took a series of deep breaths. As she did, Lisa followed the sat nav along Great Western Road, driving past the Botanic Gardens and from Woodlands Road, the Corolla merged onto the M8.

Hope, she thought. That's why I'm so agitated. Hope had crept back in like an old friend returning unannounced after a long trip overseas. Lisa didn't realise until now how much faith she had in Quinn's tenacity. The girl had never sent a text like this before. *Big news.* And not a spelling mistake in sight either, another rarity. It had to be something special, Lisa thought. And that's why she was so nervous.

Maybe after tonight she wouldn't be afraid to go home. Maybe it would even start to feel like home again and she wouldn't have a heart attack every time she opened the front door or heard the phone ring.

Don't get ahead of yourself, she thought.

The Toyota travelled west on the M8. It wasn't long before Lisa was speeding again, committing the same road thuggery that she detested from other drivers, like tailgating, zipping in and out of the lanes and almost crashing into other cars in the process. But goddammit, why was everyone driving like a learner tonight? She even beeped the horn, something she never did. They beeped back and she swore at them.

Eighty miles per hour. It still felt like a crawl.

The scent of stale smoke was overpowering. The Corolla's ashtray was fat with cigarette butts and there were plenty more on the floor next to the pedals, along with dropped crisps, biscuit fragments and other rubbish. The poor car was long overdue some TLC.

Maybe next week, Lisa thought.

She steered off the M8, driving onto Castle Street, alongside the Royal Infirmary. She glanced in the rearview mirror, grimacing at the gaunt reflection. The dark shadows, the dirty pale complexion – those were as familiar to Lisa by now as the back of her hand. It was like she'd aged ten years since Tommy's memorial. And yet there was that flicker of hope in those tired eyes. A light had come back on, one that she'd thought was extinguished.

Don't let me down Quinn, Lisa thought, turning onto

Cathedral Square. She brought the car down to cruising speed and leaned forward, noticing the outline of the Monteath Mausoleum, a familiar landmark on the upper hill of the cemetery.

Your destination is on the left.

Lisa turned off the sat nav. The car rolled to a stop and she picked up her phone off the passenger seat. She looked at Quinn's text again. It *was* unusual. The tone, the lack of spelling mistakes and for crying out loud, the girl had even used punctuation.

"Where are you?" Lisa whispered, staring through the windscreen. Quinn hadn't specified what section of the Necropolis they were supposed to meet up at. Lisa was in the dark, both literally and figuratively. The cemetery was massive. Did Quinn really expect Lisa to go walkabout in there until they bumped into one another?

Hi!

Hi!

Fancy meeting you here.

She turned the car onto a deserted Wishart St, approaching the shadowy spire of the cathedral up ahead.

This would have to do.

Lisa pulled into one of many vacant parking spaces at the edge of the road. The Bridge of Sighs, a stone-arched bridge that crossed over the Molendinar Burn and into the Necropolis, was about fifty metres in front of her.

The city was quiet tonight. Quiet for a Saturday night, at least by Glasgow standards. What sort of person would hang around the Necropolis at night? Lisa had heard some of the stories about ghosts and vampires. Of course, she didn't believe a word of it.

She didn't believe in psychics once either.

Lisa killed the engine. She felt the nagging anxiety eating away at her courage. "Where are you Quinn?"

She stared through the windscreen.

Decided it was time to get out and do something.

26

QUINN

"You die first," Ewan said to Quinn.

His stride was robotic and lumbering as he approached her from the footpath. "After that, I'm going to strangle dear old Auntie Lisa and pin it on you."

Quinn stood her ground on the strip of grass. Hoping it would throw Ewan off his murderous rhythm.

"You're going to strangle her?" she said. "Because of Tommy?"

"Sure."

Quinn pointed at Fran. "Why does she get a free pass? She's the one who put Tommy in the water. And she did nothing to help him."

Ewan's face was a blank mask, the gaze trapped on some vague focal point. It was like he wasn't really there.

"Love truly is blind," Quinn said. "Isn't it?"

She started backing away from Ewan whose murderous lizard brain continued to propel him forward. Quinn bumped into the Celtic Cross behind her and for a terrifying moment, it felt like the cemetery was boxing her in.

"Do you even have the balls to strangle anyone?" she said, trying to stall him. Trying to assess the exit strategies. The options weren't great. All roads led to darkness. The footpath was there but it was going to be difficult to follow without a torch to guide her. Cutting across the grass was a risk. It meant the possibility of tripping over countless headstones and getting injured.

"You're a coward Ewan," she said. "Nothing but a fucking coward. You told Abbey to have an abortion or you'd leave her, right? You wouldn't even go to the clinic with her. You didn't sit with her. You didn't hold her hand. Wow, she must have been messed up to choose a spineless cunt like you for a boyfriend."

"I'd be careful if I was you," Fran said. She was on the footpath, lighting Ewan's way with her torch. "You don't want to piss him off."

Quinn felt like a cornered alley cat.

"Fuck you both."

Ewan's slow pursuit exploded into a sudden charge. He slammed a hammer-like fist into the side of Quinn's face. Quinn's legs did a silly dance but she managed to stay upright.

"Coward," she hissed, her mouth filling up with blood. She spat some at Ewan's feet and held her arms out wide, inviting him to try again. "Fucking coward. Did you breathe a sigh of relief when you heard that Abbey and your baby were dead?"

"Shut your mouth bitch."

Ewan swung at her again but this time he telegraphed the shot too much. Quinn saw it coming, ducked her head out of the firing line. Then she pounced. She grabbed his giant fist with both hands and with a roar, sunk her teeth deep into the soft white flesh. His skin tasted of salt.

Ewan screamed. For a few seconds, he was paralysed by the shock and pain of Quinn's ambush.

Quinn released the bite. She ran onto the path, pumping her arms and legs as hard as she could. With the torchlight behind her, the Necropolis grew darker. It felt like she was being swallowed up by the void.

"Get her!" Ewan yelled through the pain. "Fucking get her. Don't let her find the gate."

Quinn heard the sound of someone exploding into a frantic sprint behind her. She heard heavy, panicked breathing. It sounded like a wild animal on her tail.

Don't let her find the gate.

Quinn knew that she was running for her life.

27

LISA

Lisa passed through the gate and entered the Necropolis.

From the start, it felt like the gothic hellhole was pushing her back towards the gate. Telling her to keep out. She held the iPhone's torchlight in front of her, angling the beam towards wherever her feet were about to land. The light wasn't much. It was a firefly on a stick battling against the dark side of the moon. But Lisa kept pushing forward, concerned that her battery would die and leave her trapped deep inside the cemetery without a light to guide her back to the road.

Where was Quinn? Why wasn't she answering Lisa's calls or replying to her texts?

Something was wrong. That much was obvious.

Lisa glanced to her left, saw the outline of the tall cathedral. Behind that, High Street and the city centre. Streetlights. Noise and people. Usually, Lisa wasn't drawn to crowds but it was a comforting thought right now, knowing that there were other people out there. Just a short distance away. Still, the Necropolis was a silent world, eerily set apart from everything else. Its proximity to the city centre meant nothing at this hour.

Lisa followed the footpath, sticking to the centre as it wound its way uphill into the heart of the cemetery. It was an easy walk, not particularly steep. All manner of headstones, all shapes and sizes, towered over Lisa to the right. Long and knotted branches, like monstrous arms, grabbed at her as she walked past.

"Quinn? Are you there?"

Her voice felt like an intrusion. Like she was talking in church over a funeral service.

"Quinn?"

The path curved gently to the right. Lisa continued the uphill trek, still worried about her battery running out. She decided to cut over the grass to save time. Lisa took a sharp left, hurrying onto the damp grass, walking past headstone after headstone that appeared in the torchlight. Lisa did her best not to get too close to any of them. She was about to merge back onto the path when she heard a sudden noise.

She stopped dead.

Heavy, plodding footsteps approached. For a moment, Lisa's mind reverted to that of a frightened child. She imagined ghosts and vampires dragging themselves out of their graves, crawling on all fours as they hunted for anyone foolish enough to wander around the Necropolis after dark.

"Quinn? Is that you?"

The darkness took the shape of a man. Lisa's feet were frozen to the ground, adding a third option to her deep-rooted fight or flight instinct. Stand and gawp.

She screamed.

Tommy was walking towards her. This *was* Tommy. He walked like a jungle cat. He had the same curly blond hair in death as he'd had in life. She'd been right all along. Tommy Granger was back from the dead and everyone else had been wrong to doubt her. Tommy was unable to rest. Unable to forgive Lisa for leaving him to die in the Clyde. Now he was undead and no amount of charity or acts of compensation would ever be enough to fix it.

Lisa fell onto her knees and clasped her hands together. There was no more fight left inside her. "Tommy. I'm so..."

"Auntie Lisa."

Lisa gasped. She hurried back to her feet, trying to regain her balance.

"Ewan? Is that you?"

"Aye."

"What the hell are you doing here? I thought..."

He came closer. Lisa felt a sudden stab of panic when she saw the smile on his face. She didn't recognise the look in her nephew's eyes. This wasn't Ewan, the Granger family simpleton, standing in front of her. His eyes burned with intensity. His upper lip formed a snarl that made his face unrecognisable to Lisa. Without the beanie hat that he'd worn so often, he was the spitting image of his uncle. It was as if Tommy had cloned himself.

Lisa felt a dull, sickening sensation in her stomach. "Ewan. Talk to me. What are you doing here?"

"Waiting for you."

"Ewan, what have you done?"

Ewan smiled again, baring his teeth. "You know what I've been doing, *Auntie*. Don't you?"

Lisa felt the chill of ice water flowing through her veins. She pointed the torchlight at Ewan's face and at that moment, he could have been the vengeful ghost of his uncle. Lisa's other arm remained lowered at her side, tucked behind her back.

"My God," she said. "Why?"

"You let him die down there. You made the decision to let my uncle die in the dark, stinking Clyde."

"Ewan..."

"He wasn't supposed to die," Ewan snapped. Spit flew from his mouth. Then he glared at Lisa, deep lines emerging on his forehead and around his eyes. "You could have done something."

"You're right," Lisa said. "I could have done something. And I know I made a terrible choice but..."

The sound of Ewan's hateful laughter filled her head.

"But what?"

"He was cheating on me for God's sake," Lisa said. The bite was back in her voice. "He was pissing all over our marriage, and not for the first time either. No, your family don't know that he cheated on me before but he did. I was angry with him Ewan. I was fucking furious. It's no excuse for what I did but that's how it is."

Ewan spat out another sneering laugh.

"Stupid cunt. Uncle Tommy wasn't cheating on you."

"Yes," Lisa said. "He was."

Ewan glared at Lisa.

"Abbey was *my* girlfriend," he said. "The baby was mine. Tommy was taking her to the clinic in Clydebank to get it fixed. He was doing that for me."

Lisa's body shook violently. She blinked hard, saw a vision of Tommy's face in the river. It was the same rubbery mask that had haunted her nightmares for the past year. His blond curls dancing underwater. Begging Lisa for help with his swollen eyes. Hammering on the glass with his hands and elbows.

She let out a muffled scream.

Then a voice in her head. It barked at Lisa like a drill

instructor. Told her to get a hold of herself. That this wasn't the time to process.

Ewan started walking towards her. "It's clean up time, Auntie."

She shook her head. "What?"

Ewan stopped. "We got your wee pal with the green hair at the Barrowlands. Then we brought her here. Tonight, the fun and games come to an end. We frame Quinn Hart for everything. We frame her for the letters, the phone calls, you name it. We're going to make it look like she was trolling you, bribing you for money. You've probably put money into her bank account already, aye? They'll trace that. When we're done here, I'll go to your house, destroy the letters. Then I'll type out replacements written by Quinn. Generic replacements written by a troll who just wants attention. I'll point them away from the river. Away from Fran and what really happened. That's good news for you Auntie – nobody will know that you let Tommy drown."

"You evil little fucker," Lisa said. "Who are you?"

Ewan shrugged.

"You're not well Ewan. There's something wrong with you."

Ewan wasn't listening. He was stretching out the fingers of a pair of black gloves, giving each one a firm jerk. Then he began to stretch the gloves over his hands. His face was expressionless.

"Here's what happened tonight. Quinn called you out here for a meeting. A disagreement broke out. You told her to leave you alone. Told her you wouldn't put up with it anymore. She said she was going to keep trolling you for the rest of your life. Said she'd follow you anywhere, keep reminding you about Tommy unless you paid her to lay off. There was a fight. She strangled you to death but the guilt was hard for her. The fear of punishment was too much and well…"

He looked up to the sky.

"Death by hanging. Lots of trees around here. And I've got a nice bundle of rope in the van."

Ewan rubbed his gloved hands together. The smile was back. "Looks like I'll have to play the mourning nephew again."

He started walking towards her.

Lisa lowered the torchlight. Finally, she raised her right arm, the arm she'd kept hidden at her side in the darkness. The baseball bat had seemed like a silly purchase at the time. But now, Lisa thought, revealing it to her nephew, it felt like a smart buy.

"You evil little prick," she said. "Let me give you a piece of advice. Next time you send a text from Quinn Hart, make sure you throw a few typos in there. And put it in all caps. It'll eliminate suspicion."

Lisa bent her knees, raising the bat behind her head.

"Come and get it."

28

QUINN

Quinn was lost inside the Necropolis. Every turn felt like another move in the wrong direction. All the drink, drugs and smoking hadn't prepared her for this much running uphill. Her lungs were burning, legs numb. She'd suffer for it later, that's assuming she got out alive. Right now, all her aches and pains were suppressed by the lightning bolt of adrenaline that surged through her.

She ran blind, eyes slowly adjusting to the dark.

All these headstones. The Necropolis felt more like a labyrinth than a cemetery, especially in the dark. She saw the outline of a tall mausoleum up ahead. Creepy as hell, she thought. Quinn was desperate but she could she bring herself to hide in something like that?

No, but not because it was too scary. Because Lisa was on her way. Quinn couldn't just hide and...

"FUCKING BITCH!"

The voice exploded from out of nowhere. Quinn spun around just in time to see Fran's enraged face closing the gap. Her arm was cocked back and she threw something at Quinn with full force. Quinn jerked her head out of the way, gambling on which direction to duck. The rock whistled past her right ear.

She didn't have time to breathe a sigh of relief.

Fran rugby-tackled Quinn to the path, landing on top of her with all the weight of a full-grown grizzly bear. Quinn fell hard on her back and the impact put her out for a split second. She came back to, blinking off the short sleep. The two women rolled over the concrete, locked in each other's grip. Fran was the first to break free and she pounced on Quinn like a wildcat. She mounted her, pinned her to the path. Then she began to rake at Quinn's eyes with her nails. Hissing. Cursing. Spitting. Most of the blows missed the target but Quinn did feel a sharp fingernail slicing into the skin below the right eye. Fran was trying to blind her. Quinn closed her eyes, fighting desperately from the bottom. She threw a series of wild slaps and punches and the ones that landed had no real weight behind them. Meanwhile, Fran's claw-like nails continued to carve her face open. Quinn could feel the hot blood cascading down her face.

Fran was built like a toothpick but she was fast and surprisingly strong. Her verbal insults landed with the same intensity as the physical blows.

"Fuckingbitchfuckingbitchfuckingbitchfuckingbitch!"

Quinn tried to grab Fran by the arms. Tried to lock her up, stifle the assault. Those lean, wiry muscles had to be filling up with lactic acid by now, Quinn figured. And when Fran slowed down, maybe Quinn could use her weight to push her off. But so far, Fran was relentless in her attack. Quinn gave up on the arms and tried to grab the girl's fingers instead. Get one, isolate it. Bend it all the way back till the joint snapped.

But Quinn couldn't get anything off. Fran was possessed and fighting as if her life depended on it. It was Quinn that was slowing down. All that running uphill. Her limbs felt like two lead blocks.

"Fuckingbitchfuckingbitchfuckingbitchfuckingbitch!"

Quinn had one idea left. She slipped her left hand inside the pocket of her jeans. Doing this left one side of her face unguarded, open to Fran's vicious attack from the top. Quinn took the blows, wincing and hoping she wouldn't pass out or go blind in one eye. She rummaged around in her pocket, pulled out the hard guitar pick, the only thing that Ewan hadn't removed from her pockets when she'd been out cold. Rocking her body from side to side, Quinn managed to knock Fran off-balance. She did it again and Fran's solid base wobbled. Quinn used this window of opportunity to stretch her right arm over her body and with that hand, she slotted the pick in between the closed fingers of her left hand, leaving the narrow tip exposed at the knuckles.

She fell back. Closed her left hand into a tight fist and waited.

Fran's assault *had* slowed. The girl's attack was sloppy at best as Quinn lay bleeding underneath her. After winding up another punch, Fran left her right arm hanging in the air. Just a second too long. Quinn saw it. She exploded upwards, putting everything into the punch. The blow landed flush, the sharp tip of the guitar pick slicing into Fran's fleshy eyeball.

Fran's bloodcurdling scream was loud enough to wake up the dead. She toppled to the side, both hands pressed over the injured eye.

"Bitch!" she yelled. "I'll fucking kill you."

Both women climbed back to their feet. They staggered towards one another.

Quinn was first on the draw this time. She threw a snappy kick to the chest that sent Fran hurtling off the footpath. Fran backpedalled, reversing faster than her legs could handle. She tripped over a flat headstone. Quinn winced at the sound of the girl's head cracking off a marble slab.

Fran lay still beside the grave. Unconscious.

"Jesus," Quinn said, dabbing at the scratches on her face. Her skin felt like it had gone up against a blowtorch. She was about to collapse onto her knees when she heard a woman's scream from elsewhere inside the Necropolis.

"No," she said.

Quinn began to stagger in the scream's direction.

"Lisa."

29

QUINN

Quinn snatched Fran's phone off the path as she set off downhill in search of Lisa. As she ran, she activated the torch and pointed it ahead of her.

She was in bad shape. Blood and sweat continued to pour down her face. The cemetery was spinning around like a fairground attraction speeding up to a dangerous speed. Marauding headstones leapt out at Quinn as she skipped off the footpath and cut over the grass. It felt like the headstones had arms. Long, blurry arms that were grabbing at her.

Quinn didn't have much left in the tank. She was running on reserves by now, a dry sponge that couldn't be squeezed any more. As her frantic descent in the Necropolis accelerated to a manic speed, it felt more like flying than running.

"Lisa?"

She cut over another path. Vaulted a short fence, half-expecting to fall and faceplant on the concrete. Running downhill again.

"Lisa?"

Quinn stopped at the edge of the grass. There was a flicker of movement beside a cluster of headstones up ahead. She wiped the sweat out of her eyes. Took deep gulps of air to slow her runaway heart.

There it was again. Someone was up to something under one of those big Celtic Crosses that were so prevalent in the cemetery.

Quinn tiptoed across the path, stepping quietly onto the grass. She kept the torch low, its light pointing towards the ground. She strained her eyes. Realised with a sinking feeling that she was looking at a man standing over something on the ground.

Not something. Someone.

No.

Quinn closed the gap further. She couldn't stop her heart drumming off her ribcage.

It was Ewan. He was squatting over the motionless form of Lisa. Quinn saw the black gloves covering his hands. Oh shit, she thought. Was she too late? When Ewan turned his head to the side for a brief second, Quinn noticed a nasty-looking gash around his eye.

She smiled.

Attagirl.

The smile fizzled out as she watched Ewan wrap his fingers around Lisa's throat. He leaned into his aunt. His arms began to tremble. All Quinn could see now was the back of his head. But she could imagine the blank look in his eyes.

There was no time to lose.

Quinn was no match for him. But she wasn't about to let Lisa die in the hands of a monster. Even though she could. Even though she could run now and save herself. She was about to charge at Ewan when she noticed a glint of metal winking at her from the grass. The object, whatever it was, was about ten feet behind Ewan who was so absorbed in the act of murdering his aunt that he hadn't noticed Quinn creeping up at his back.

It was a baseball bat.

"Now you know," Ewan said to his dying aunt. He spoke in a cold, matter-of-fact voice. "Now you know what it's like to long for air."

He tightened the stranglehold.

Lisa let out a gargled coughing noise.

Quinn abandoned the torch. She picked up the bat and curled her fingers around the aluminium handle.

She ran forward.

Ewan's head spun around at the sudden disturbance from behind. He jumped to his feet and squinted. "What the fuck? Fran, is that you?"

Quinn leapt out of the darkness. She swung the bat and the barrel cracked off Ewan's skull with a satisfying pop. He cried out, backpedalled away with his limbs doing a strange octopus dance. Quinn wasn't about to let him recover. She pursued her prey relentlessly, hitting him again, once, twice, three times. Ewan flopped to his knees. He made a noise that sounded like a large animal's death cry. He toppled over onto his back and Quinn, not about to take any chances, cracked him on the skull again. She didn't let up until Ewan was out cold.

"Sleep tight," she said, standing over him. By now, her face was a bloody, burning mess.

Quinn dropped the bat. She fell onto her knees beside Lisa.

"Lisa," she said, shaking the woman hard. "Lisa, can you hear me? C'mon, talk to me."

She gasped. Lisa's face had recently been used as a punching bag. One side was badly swollen, looked like a hematoma coming up on the forehead. A trail of blood fell from Lisa's nose and mouth. At least, Quinn thought, Lisa had given Ewan something to think about with that gash over the eye.

"Wake up Lisa."

Quinn shook her again. Lisa's eyes slowly opened and after a muffled cough, she wriggled around furiously on the grass as if the attack was still taking place. As if Ewan was still on top of her. "No...no, stop!"

Quinn grabbed her by the arms. "Hey. It's okay. It's me, it's Quinn."

"Quinn...?"

"Aye, I don't look so hot at the moment. Neither do you. But you're going to be okay. It's over."

"Ewan...?"

"Ewan's consciousness has left the building," Quinn said. "Don't worry about him."

Lisa's bottom lip began to tremble. She tried to sit up but Quinn held her firmly in place, not sure if moving her was a good idea or not. But Lisa was stubborn. It looked like she wanted to say something. Quinn shook her head, pressing her bloody fingers over Lisa's warm lips.

She smiled.

"Save your strength. You're going to need it when I send you the bill."

TWO WEEKS LATER

30

QUINN

"She's gone you say?"

The old woman lifted up her glasses and leaned forward in the velvet armchair. She lifted the remote control off her lap and after examining the buttons, turned off the TV. Until that moment, a romantic comedy starring Julia Roberts had been playing at low volume in the background. Now Julia was gone and there was only a puzzled look on the woman's wrinkled face.

"Lisa's gone?"

"That's right," Quinn said, sitting on the other armchair, hands tightly clasped together. She was smiling but the old dear had the radiator set to furnace mode. Quinn was melting under her frayed denim jacket and ripped jeans. So far at least, she hadn't passed out. The situation reminded Quinn of her own grandmother, the woman who'd brought her up in Dollar after her mother's sudden death. She was always cold. That woman would have been cold inside the heart of the sun, that's what Quinn's granddad used to say.

"She moved out last week."

Annette glanced at the TV. She shook her head, looked at Quinn. There was a hint of confusion in her eyes.

"Who...?"

"Lisa," Quinn said. "Your last caring caller. She moved out of her house last week."

"Oh yes," Annette said, her blue eyes lighting up. It was like a switch had been turned back on. "I do remember her talking about moving. But that *is* sudden. What about her house? What about her job? She's a..."

"Vet."

"Aye, that's right. What about all that?"

"She's working on those things," Quinn said. "But she decided to make the leap first and deal with the admin from afar. She's hired people to help her out with all the details. So I've been told. Seems like everything can be done online these days."

Annette's face was steeped in concentration. The old chair groaned as she leaned back. "Where did she go?"

Quinn shrugged. "Down south."

"Has she got a new job then?"

"I don't know that either," Quinn said, following instructions to remain as vague as possible. "Like I said, she's working on it."

Annette studied Quinn's face without any sense of embarrassment. She'd already gawped at the green hair and ripped jeans when Quinn arrived at the door. Now she was examining the jagged scars mapping both sides of the young woman's face. The scars had faded but were still clearly visible.

"That looks sore. What happened?"

"Stray cat," Quinn said, riffing out the same old line

she'd given everyone else. "He tried to turn me into a scratching post."

"Cat? Bloody tiger more like."

Quinn's polite smile remained intact.

It was a busy couple of weeks following the events of the Necropolis. No one had been busier during that time than Lisa Granger. Despite getting beat up and almost strangled to death, she hadn't gone to the hospital. Quinn and Lisa had staggered through the cemetery gate, bleeding and sore. Quinn still had Fran's mobile phone and she used it make an anonymous call to the emergency services, informing them that two people were badly injured inside the Necropolis. After dumping the phone (as well as the baseball bat), Quinn had driven the Corolla back to Lisa's house. They'd cleaned up, treated their wounds (no small task) and Quinn spent the night on the couch, loaded up on painkillers. They'd parted company in the morning. After that, there was only the occasional phone call between them. On that first call, Lisa told Quinn that she'd arranged a hasty exit out of Glasgow. Ewan was in a coma, according to the Grangers. He'd been assaulted during a night out in town and there'd been some bleeding on the brain. Quinn received a follow-up text from Lisa two days later, informing her that Ewan was now awake. That he was recovering.

Lisa didn't know anything about Fran's whereabouts since that night. Quinn decided to ask around and heard from one of Donnie's acquaintances that the majority of travellers in Newton Mearns had moved on. Quinn's gut instinct told her that Fran had gone with them. That she'd done a runner before the police came knocking on her caravan door. Even if that meant leaving Ewan behind.

There were only a couple of tasks left for Quinn to perform on Lisa's behalf. One of those was to keep Lisa's final caring caller visit with Annette. Lisa wanted Quinn to thank the old woman for all she'd done to help Lisa. Quinn was also to reassure Annette that others, specifically Deb and Risha, would be taking her place.

Quinn's final task was to visit Ewan in the Royal Infirmary. She'd do whatever it took to make contact with the psycho. When she had him alone, Quinn was to inform Ewan that Lisa was willing to stay quiet if he was. It was a simple trade – silence for silence. Ewan was never to speak about how Lisa left Tommy in the water. If Ewan so much as whispered anything inappropriate, Lisa would send the voice recording she'd made in the Necropolis to Iris Granger. As well as the police.

The voice recording didn't exist. But Lisa and Quinn were willing to gamble that Ewan wasn't willing to take the risk.

It was a stalemate and that was the best they could do.

Quinn felt her phone vibrating in her pocket.

"Lisa had a lot on her mind this past year," she said, picking up an Oreo cookie from the plate of biscuits on the coffee table. It still hurt to chew but Quinn was starving.

"Skin and bones," Annette said, nodding her head slowly. "The poor thing's nothing but skin and bones. Her husband's loss really affected her. I wish she had a fraction of your appetite."

"She'll be okay," Quinn said. "She's tougher than she looks. And she told me she's been putting weight back on ever since she left Glasgow."

Annette sighed. She picked up the remote control, aiming it at the TV.

"Do you want to watch the rest of *Notting Hill*? It's got Julia Roberts and Hugh Grant in it."

"I'd love to," Quinn said, grabbing a handful of cookies

off the plate and making herself comfortable in the armchair.

They watched the film to its conclusion. When the credits rolled forty-five minutes later, Quinn got to her feet and stretched her arms out. "Time I was going."

"Aye, no problem sweetheart."

Annette gripped the armrests, preparing to stand up. "Do you want me to give you some cream for your face? I get it from Boots. It's got Aloe Vera in it."

"No thanks," Quinn said, signalling for Annette to stay in her seat. "I've got enough skin cream to last me ten years."

"Ye sure hen?"

"Aye," Quinn said, pausing in the living room doorway. "Now, is there anything I can do for you before I go? I can do the washing up. Help you to bed?"

Annette waved the offer away. She grabbed the remote control off the armrest and studied the buttons again. "Och, I'll be fine darling. Think I'll stay up for a while, eh? There's another film coming on that I want to watch. It's got Elizabeth Taylor and Richard Burton in it. You probably don't know who they are. Eh?"

"Sure I do," Quinn said, grinning. "They're in *Who's Afraid of Virginia Woolf* together. It's one of my favourite films."

Annette was back to gawping at Quinn's ripped jeans. "What was that love?"

Quinn waved. "Nothing. Take care Annette."

She closed the door behind her and stepped out into a cool, damp evening. Quinn began the short walk to the bus stop, typing out a text to Lisa, letting her know that Annette was okay and wished her all the best for the future. She also wrote a quick follow up text informing Lisa that she was heading to the Royal Infirmary.

She finished up with a smiley face.

In a few days, Quinn would delete Lisa's number. Their working relationship was almost over and the two women would never talk again. Quinn knew that Lisa had to cut all ties with Glasgow. She had to start looking forward instead of back and a big part of that was coming to terms with what really happened in the river.

That wouldn't be easy. But Quinn had faith in Lisa's ability to tame the beast.

She was about to slip the phone into her pocket when it vibrated again. How many times was that? Six? Seven? Stepping underneath the bus shelter, Quinn checked the timetable on the wall. She had a six-minute wait for the next bus that would take her to High Street. From there, it was a short walk to the hospital.

With a tired sigh, she sat down on the cold bench. Quinn checked her phone. As she thought, it was vibrating because of the news notifications she'd subscribed to earlier in the day.

A breaking story had caught her attention.

A murder in London.

Reports were still vague and new information was coming in all the time. A forty-seven-year-old woman had been murdered in her home in Islington. Nothing unusual about a murder in London, Quinn thought. Except the woman wasn't part of any criminal organisation and she didn't seem to have any enemies that anyone in her inner circle could think of. She was a working professional, a mother of two young children with a nice, middle-class life.

There was no motive.

And yet she'd been bludgeoned to death with a sledgehammer.

Quinn reread the description of the killer. It was a brief

flurry of details provided by the dead woman's neighbour. Quinn zoned in on one part in particular. The neighbour told the police he'd seen a heavyset man in a balaclava running out of the house.

A heavyset man in a balaclava.

There was no mention of The Hammer killings in Scotland. It wasn't in any of the reports. Too soon for them, Quinn thought. It was too soon to make the connection.

Not for her.

The bus growled as it approached from afar. Two massive headlights appeared as the single-decker turned the final corner before the stop.

Quinn stared at her phone, lost in thought. How long had it been since the Lenzie murder, the last of The Hammer killings? Sixteen years. And now here was this new lookalike slaying four hundred miles south of here, a crime that mirrored exactly what six-year-old Quinn had witnessed in the big house.

Of course, it could be a coincidence.

It *had* to be a coincidence.

When she looked up, the bus was gone. Quinn shrugged. She made herself comfortable on the bench, then went back online, doing what any other good PI would do in a situation like this one. She was asking the only question that mattered.

How much was a flight to London?

THE END

OTHER THRILLER/SUSPENSE BOOKS BY MARK GILLESPIE

Three men are kidnapped on the eve of their high school reunion and wake up trapped inside a remote cabin in the Scottish Highlands.

What comes next is the discovery that one of them is a killer.

The Old Boys

The starlet and the starmaker. It's an age-old story in Hollywood. Now that story's about to be rewritten. In blood.

Scream Test

Mike Harvey just broke up with his girlfriend. Now her daddy, the Devil, is coming after him. And Daddy's mad as Hell.

Devil in the Dark Woods

POST APOCALYPTIC/DYSTOPIAN TITLES BY MARK GILLESPIE

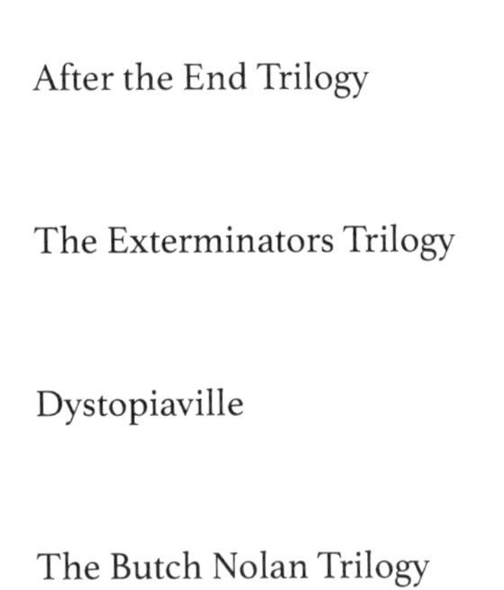

After the End Trilogy

The Exterminators Trilogy

Dystopiaville

The Butch Nolan Trilogy

Mark Gillespie's author website
www.markgillespieauthor.com

Mark Gillespie on Facebook
www.facebook.com/markgillespieswritingstuff

Mark Gillespie on Twitter
www.twitter.com/MarkG_Author

Mark Gillespie on Bookbub
https://www.bookbub.com/profile/mark-gillespie